READER PRAIS
SERIES

"I love this series. ⸻ my favorite authors. I think everyone will enjoy this series. The 3 friends are very hard not to love." ~ Amazon Reviewer

"I loved it. The way he loved her, strong chemistry between them. This is a great series 🖤 🧡 beautiful." ~ Amazon Reviewer

"I truly enjoyed every book in this series and I can't wait to read more from this author." ~ Amazon Reviewer

ALSO BY KIRU TAYE

Men of Valor series:
His Treasure
His Strength
His Princess
Her Protector
Men of Valor box set (books 1 – 3)

The Essien Series:
Keeping Secrets
Making Scandal
Riding Rebel
Kola
A Very Essien Christmas
Freddie Entangled
Freddie Untangled

The Bound Series:
Bound to Fate
Bound to Ransom
Bound to Passion
Bound to Favor
Bound to Liberty

The Challenge Series:
Valentine
Engaged
Worthy
Captive

The Yadili Series:
Prince of Hearts
Killer of Kings
Bad Santa
Rough Diamond
Tough Alliance
Honour (featured in Love and The Lawless anthology)

PNR / Fantasy romance
Outcast
Sacrifice
Black Soul
Scar's Redemption
Haunted (featured in Enchanted: Volume Two anthology)

The Ben & Selina Trilogy
Scars,
Secrets
Scores

The Royal House of Saene Series:
His Captive Princess
Saving Her Guard
The Tainted Prince
The Future King
The Future Queen
Screwdriver

Viva City FC Series:
Tapping Up
Against the Run of Play

Kiru Taye

Captive
CHALLENGE #4

Captive

First Published in Great Britain in 2021 by
LOVE AFRICA PRESS
103 Reaver House, 12 East Street, Epsom KT17 1HX
www.loveafricapress.com

Home of African Love Stories

ISBN: 978-1-914226-58-8
Also available in eBook

Blurb

With her BFF and ex-lover now happily engaged to the man of her dreams, Anuli Okoro is left to her own devices. She's accepted that there can never be a fairy tale ending for her. She's too damaged to ever fit with anyone else.

Until she pushes too far and lands herself in hot water with Tope Balogun, an annoyingly sexy man who sees the darkness inside her and isn't fazed by it. Fighting him doesn't work because he seems to know her too well.

She has plans to deal with her dark past, and the only option is to escape before Tope totally consumes her.

Author's Note

Dear Readers,

Thank you for your love for the Challenge series. I'm kind of sad to write the last story to a series that started back in 2012. As you know, it was initially going to be three books. But Anuli had such a prominent role in Book 3, and she really needed closure on the issues surrounding her past, which is how Book 4 was born.

However, I should mention that this story is not a conventional romance. It is erotic suspense. Anuli is not your average girl next door. She needed a man who wasn't looking to change her into a 'conventional' woman. I hope you agree with me when you read the story that Tope is that man she needs.

I hope you enjoy this adventure of a story. Be sure to visit my website and sign up to my mailing list for news about the next book release.

Love,
Kiru xx

Kiru Taye

Chapter One

"Did you hear what happened to my neighbours?"

Anuli couldn't see the person speaking. She stood in a closed cubicle in the ladies' toilet, hands on the sliding lock, ready to open it.

Pausing, she tilted her head to the side, left ear close to the wooden slab separating her from the women chatting by the sinks.

"No. What happened?" a second girl asked. Unlike the first lady, whose voice sounded nasal as if she had a cold, this one's tone had a warm rasp to it.

"You won't believe it." The first girl lowered her voice. Anuli pictured her leaning close to the other girl to speak. "My neighbour's wife reported him to the police. Apparently, he had sex with their daughter."

"Tufiakwa!" the second woman exclaimed.

Anuli's stomach congealed. Nausea rose, leaving a bitter taste in her mouth. For a brief moment, she was that little girl with her stepfather's weight crushing her body, his sweaty scent in her nostrils. She gulped in air, shaking her head to chase the memory away. She needed to get out of here. The ongoing conversation stopped her.

"That's not the worst of it. The police arrested the man but sent him back home without any charges. They said it was a domestic and civil matter. So the man went back to the house to continue abusing his daughter. Can you imagine?"

"Oh my God! No!"

The sound of running water stopped with the squeak of the taps.

"Yes, o. So the woman *jejely* poisoned her husband to death. The police showed up and arrested her."

"Oh no! That's not right."

"The police could have prevented this from happening. Now they are punishing the girl twice. She's a victim, and now she doesn't even have her mother because the woman is in police lock-up."

"What nonsense. The woman needs a good lawyer."

Heels tapped on the hard flooring. Hinges creaked.

"Yes, she does. Some of the neighbours got together and found a lawyer for her. Hopefully, she'll be out on bail soon."

"Good. This kind of nonsense has to stop..." The woman's voice faded as a door slammed shut. Both ladies had left the restroom.

Anuli braced her hands against the wooden partition, gulping in breath to ease the tension in her body. Her initial repulsion against the man's paedophilia had morphed to anger when she'd found out the man hadn't been charged and his wife was now in jail.

The story almost mirrored what had happened to her as a child. Except her mother had died, and her abuser was still alive.

She jerked the toilet door open. It slammed against the wall as she strode up to a sink. Dumping her bag on the counter, she took tissues from the dispenser and dabbed the sweat from her forehead. Her eyes blazed with fury in the mirror.

Why did this kind of shit keep happening, and the people who should protect the vulnerable not do anything about it?

She washed her fidgety hands and switched off the tap before snatching her purse and heading for the exit. She walked into the bar. 'Ada Ada' by Flavour greeted her from hidden speakers, the music low enough for rumbling conversations to be overheard. The lounge had filled up since she went to the restroom.

Regina, a slim girl with dark-brown skin and close-cropped hair, moved her bag to make space for Anuli on the stool she'd vacated earlier. "You're back."

Nodding, Anuli waved at the bar man and climbed onto the chair. She needed a strong drink, something to wipe out the memories that had resurfaced. She tapped her fingertips on the shiny hard black surface of the counter.

"Are you okay?" Regina asked, lifting her glass to mocha lips.

Anuli looked up and forced a smile on her face. She didn't discuss her past with people, and she certainly wouldn't start now, although Regina was a friend. "I'm fine. I just need a drink."

Regina's lips curled upward at the corners. She reminded Anuli of Lupita Nyong'o. She had the same pretty grin on her oval face. When she tilted her head, the oversized silver loop earring matching her silver and black dress glinted in the light.

"What can I get you?" The barman, a twenty-something-year-old with a stud earring in the left ear, black shirt and trousers, beamed a smile at her. He'd been flirting with them since they arrived. Well, mainly with Regina. If he only knew she wasn't interested in men. At least, not the way he expected.

Anuli's smile bloomed at the thought, and she winked at him. "Jack Daniels and a splash of Coke."

The bartender's grin widened. "Coming right up."

He took her money, dropped it in the till and gave her change. Reaching for the liquor bottle standing on a shelf against the mirrored wall, he swivelled and poured a shot into a clean glass filled with ice before topping it off with Coke. He slid the filled glass as well as the bottle of Coke across to her.

"Do you want some?" Anuli asked the girl sitting next to her.

Regina wrinkled her nose. "No. You know I don't drink alcohol."

Shrugging, Anuli downed her drink in successive gulps. Warmth slid down her throat and across her chest. The alcoholic buzz kicked in, taking her tension away. She poured some of the remaining Coke into the glass with the tinkling ice and topped off Regina's drink with the rest.

"I'm just heading outside for a smoke," Regina said as she got off the barstool. The girl never got drunk, but she smoked cigarettes. *Go figure that one out.*

Anuli would own up to three vices—booze, nicotine and sex. Why the hell not? She wasn't looking to live to a grand old age. Just wanted to get through life the best way she could.

"I'll come with you." She stepped down as someone brushed past her, distracting her. She caught a whiff of bergamot and spices. The scent cut straight to the bone. She froze, her gaze darting around, trying to find the source.

A thrill of excitement and a shiver of terror shimmied down her spine simultaneously. The bar was full of people, sweat and smoke being the primary smells in the warm air. So why did this particular fragrance get her attention?

Just as quickly as she'd sniffed it, the scent was gone. She couldn't recapture it no matter how she tried.

"Anuli, are you coming?" Regina grabbed her attention again as she dragged two top fingers back and forth in front of her pouted lips as if she was taking a drag on a cigarette. "Smokes."

"Yes," she replied and grabbed her purse as she followed. They headed towards the exit.

The two of them had been friends for a while, but they'd started hanging out together recently.

13

The girl was bold, beautiful. Daring. She didn't have the same hang-ups as her BFF.

Mind you, she wasn't Tessa. No one could replace Tessa. What she'd shared with her best friend was remarkable. Tessa had moved on to better things with Peter. Anuli was pleased for her.

But she couldn't sit around moping about the loss of her confidante and lover. She had to move on.

Regina was the next best thing. She wasn't much of a talker, though.

That was one thing Anuli missed about Tessa's absence.

Tessa had been talkative. From the first day they'd met as kids, Anuli had been attracted to the smart girl with big words that had been Tessa. She'd been bookish and nerdy, always having something to say. Tessa hid her pain behind her sassy mouth.

Anuli didn't really know all that much about Regina. She knew the girl liked to party. They shared the same vices. For now, that was enough. She didn't need the same level of deep, dark secrets that she'd shared with Tessa.

Tessa hated that Anuli smoked. With Regina, she didn't have to worry about anyone nagging her about the hazards of cigarettes.

They pushed through the boisterous revellers. A young man staggered out of the way when she tapped his shoulder, giving her a leering smile. Another clutched a glass of blue drink precariously and would perhaps spill it on the next unsuspecting partygoer if not careful.

Her platform high heels tapped on the hard flooring as she avoided a man whose roving hand groped her bum. She caught the scent again and stiffened, gaze sweeping the space.

It could have come from anyone. Perhaps it was the beautiful girl in a short red dress whose curly braids bounced as she walked or the man wearing dark sunglasses in a dimly lit bar.

Anuli snorted. Why did people do that? She had the mind to tell him those things were called 'sunshades' for a reason.

But her heart stuttered because she'd found the source of the scent. Knew it as soon as her gaze fell upon the brick wall of a man in dark trousers and T-shirt standing close to the exit. Yes, she recognised the shiny bald head, full lips, powerful chin and a trimmed beard.

Even more telling, the heat from his eyes, as black as pitch, threatened to scorch her skin as he tracked her movement. His piercing gaze undressed her and covered her up at the same time.

Tope Balogun, head of security at Park Hotels.

Shit. Her mouth dried out, and she swallowed. She'd pictured those large, strong hands holding her down while he fucked her so hard, the bed rattled and disturbed the neighbours.

Her footsteps faltered, and she grabbed Regina, stopping her forward motion.

There was only one way out of here, and it stood right next to him. She couldn't walk out without him noticing her, even though he seemed in conversation with another man standing next to him.

Her breath locked tight in her chest, and she forced air into her lungs with a slow inhale.

"What's the matter?" Regina asked, turning her head to look at Anuli.

"Is there another way out of here?" Anuli asked in a low voice but still loud enough to be heard with the music.

"None, aside from the emergency exit. Touching that will get us arrested."

"True." She had no business getting the police involved. Anyway, what was likely to happen to her here? She was in a busy bar. And he wouldn't dare cause trouble.

If he wanted to look at her, that was his headache, not hers.

"It's okay. Let's go." She nudged Regina.

Just as she sashayed past the man, spicy fragrance filled her nostrils—a warm, firm palm wrapped around her wrist.

Her pulse thundered. She tugged, turned and glared at him.

He didn't release her as he stepped through the open door into the quiet hallway. The smile on his face didn't waver as he lowered his head, bringing his face close to hers. Warm air from his breath whispered on her cheek.

She shivered as heat settled between her legs and her knees weakened. She couldn't breathe. Couldn't speak.

He stood close enough to kiss, and if he closed the space between them, she wouldn't resist his lips on hers.

"You haven't been to work at Park Hotel for a few weeks," he said in a voice tinged with a Yoruba accent.

"I took time off for my exams." It was a lame excuse as exams finished weeks ago, but she stuck to it. Anyway, what did he care if she went to work or not? He wasn't her boss.

"Your exams ended a while ago. Your school is on break," he replied in the deep voice that sent her pulse skittering.

She sucked a sharp breath, unable to look away from his dark eyes hooded under the slash of thick brows defining his proportioned features.

"How do you know?"

"I know." His gaze didn't waver.

Her stomach did a somersault as an arc of energy tightened between them like a stretched rubber band ready to snap. Just as it had the first day she'd met him.

"Why is it your business? You don't own the hotel." She needed to get a grip. She wasn't a swooning virgin, for goodness' sake.

His full lips curled in a smirk before he grazed the lobe of her ear with his lips, sending her pulse rate through the roof. "I don't own Park Hotel, but I'm going to own your beautiful behind if you don't get back to work there."

Fingers grazed her right bum cheek as if for emphasis.

Her breath hitched, and her mouth dropped open. She tried to ignore the pulsing core at the images his words conjured. At the liberties he took. "What?"

"You heard me." He winked at her and let go of her hand. "See you soon, Tiger."

She glared at him some more and staggered out of the building into the warm breezy night, clutching her tingling wrist.

He'd just threatened her. The hard-ass, delicious-looking chief of security for Park Hotel had just threatened to own her ass.

And why did the idea make her body flush with heat and her insides clench tight?

An image of his smirking face loomed in her mind.

Damn him! Damn the sexy bastard.

She gulped in air as she stomped over to where Regina leaned against the wall, a lit cigarette between her lips. She pulled the cig from the girl's mouth, placed it to her lips and took a long drag. Tilting her head to the side, she blew out smoke from the corner of her mouth. Smoke curled around them and dissipated into the humid night.

Instead of giving Regina back the fag, she leaned forward and covered her lips in a kiss. Regina was soft and sweet. She let out a small moan as Anuli moved close and brought their bodies together, deepening the smooch.

What Anuli really wanted was a big, strong body holding her down and screwing her to oblivion. She could go back into the bar, guaranteed she'd been walking away with a man of her choice.

But Tope was still in there, and she didn't want to see his smirking face again if she could help it.

She couldn't forget the first day she'd met him in Peter Oranye's penthouse when she'd been ordered to work in the housekeeping department of the Park Hotel. Peter had instructed her to be locked in the guardhouse if she failed to comply with his instructions. Tope had stood over her like a sentry, ensuring she obeyed the order. Throughout the day, he'd been close by, watching her although he hadn't said anything to her.

In the few days that she'd worked there, they hadn't said much to each other. But there had been moments when he'd caught her staring at his body. He'd smirked at her much like he'd done tonight.

She came up for air, breaking the kiss.

"Let's go back to mine," she said to Regina. She needed to channel this desire coursing in her veins.

"Sure," the girl replied and pushed off the wall, slinging the strap of her bag over her left shoulder.

Anuli passed her hand through Regina's arm, and they sashayed to the pavement to hail a taxi. It wasn't too late in the evening, and one stopped after only a few minutes.

They got inside and sat in the back together. Anuli held onto Regina, stroking her arms. Regina leaned back against her, leaning her head on Anuli's shoulder.

Anuli didn't want to attract attention from the cab driver; otherwise, she would have pulled Regina closer for another kiss. But she didn't want to risk being kicked out of the cab.

Nigerians had enough problems with public displays of affection without adding two women kissing into the mix.

For her, it was no biggie. She loved the softness of a woman's curves as much as she loved the hardness of a man's body. Yes, she was bisexual. It wasn't about choosing one over the other. Or that she hated men, which was what some people thought. It was just the way she was made.

She was tactile and felt at ease when she had physical contact with others. Perhaps that was why she enjoyed sex so much as opposed to Tessa, who only used to do it out of necessity. To survive.

That had been before Peter. He'd given Tessa her first orgasm by a man, and Tessa hadn't looked back since.

Anuli had a consolation, though. She'd been Tessa's only female lover.

Anuli, on the other hand, wasn't ashamed to admit that she enjoyed sex. Got a kick out of it. She'd always wanted more. The next orgasm. The next high. Of course, if the men wanted to pay to fuck her, even better. That way, she wouldn't have to put up with another man who would enslave her like Uncle Joe had done.

Her body stiffened as it always did when she thought about that motherfucker. Anger boiled in her veins. The man deserved to be carved up and left to the vultures.

She hadn't thought about him for a long time. Mainly because she hadn't wanted to upset Tessa. But now, Tessa was okay, under Peter's care; she didn't have to worry about her friend anymore.

The conversations she'd overheard in the restrooms, describing what had happened to the abused girl and her family, had resurrected old emotions Anuli had kept under wraps for years. Now Anuli was left to imagine all the possible things she could do to the man who had been her tormentor if she ever got her hands on him again.

"Nuli, come on," Regina's voice roused her from her churning thoughts.

She'd been so engrossed, she hadn't realised the taxi had stopped in front of the gates of the compound that housed her rented room.

Regina pushed open the door and stepped out. Anuli followed as her friend paid the driver. She walked up to the side gate and tapped on it. She heard the cab drive off as Regina came to stand beside her. The orange light of the street lamp gave her friend an ethereal glow.

Desire sparked again in Anuli's belly, rising to mix with the ebbing fury in her veins. She grabbed Regina's wrist and shoved her against the wall, pushing her knee between the girl's thighs, forcing them apart as her skirt rode up her hips.

Regina gasped, her eyes glazing over, her mouth falling open.

Anuli took advantage and thrust her tongue inside the warm mouth just as she grabbed her nape, pulling them together. Her right hand grabbed Regina's left breast and squeezed.

Anuli was aggressive. Rough. But Regina didn't seem to mind as a moan spilled out and her body bowed off the wall. She humped Anuli's thigh wedged between hers.

Heat and dampness seeped from Regina's panties onto her bare skin.

Shuffling footsteps sounded on the other side of the wall, followed by a grating sound as a metal bolt was pulled back.

Anuli broke the kiss, panting as she whispered, "I want to fuck you tonight."

They'd kissed before, but they'd never gone all the way. Regina had been with a woman before. She'd had a girlfriend, but they'd recently broken up.

A big smile curled Regina's lips before she responded. "About time."

"Aunty, you don come back," the gateman's voice stopped Anuli from responding.

"Oga gateman, thank you." She took her friend's hand, pulling her through the open archway.

"You no bring anything for me?" the man asked as she walked past him.

They had an arrangement for him to open the gates for her when she came back late in the evenings. But she couldn't stop right now to rummage through her purse for some cash for him.

"Me and you go talk for morning, eh. No vex," she said and carried on walking.

"Okay. Good night." The sound of the man locking the gates followed her.

Anuli hurried down the side of the main two-level, cream-coloured building, where the landlord and his family lived. She needed to reach her room so she could get her hands fully on Regina without interruptions.

Stepping onto the veranda, she reached into the side of her purse and pulled out her jingling keys. Then she opened the brown wooden door. She flicked on the switch on the wall, grateful that there wasn't a power cut. Bright white light filled the room, making her squint after the gloom of the outdoors.

Regina strode past her and slumped on the low bed, pulling off her shoes.

Anuli walked over to the small reading table and flicked on the desk lamp before switching off the overhead light. She preferred the intimate feel of the dimly lit room.

Regina was already stripping off, not waiting for Anuli's instruction. The girl was beautiful, no doubt about it. She was a slim girl with dark chocolate skin and a very short afro.

Warmth spread over Anuli's skin as she watched. Anticipation made her rush to remove her clothes too. She opened the wardrobe and rummaged in one bag under the hanging clothes before pulling out the item she wanted. It was a black, double-ended silicone dildo with a leather strap-on belt. Both ends were ridged and veined like erect dicks but with one side longer than the other.

"Have you ever used this before?" she asked.

Regina's smile only widened as she spread herself on the bed, flawless dark skin on display. "Not exactly like that but similar."

"Good." Anuli climbed onto the bed. Just seeing Regina naked and waiting had her body curling tight from all the banked up desire.

Soon, she was caressing and stroking the woman's body, fingers in her wet pussy, mouth clamped around her firm breast.

"Ohhh," Regina cried out and bucked as she climaxed, her channel contracting around Anuli's digits.

Anuli couldn't wait any longer. Her body was primed. She inserted the short end of the dildo into her already soaked sex and gasped as it filled her. Then she clasped the belt over her hips. Kneeling between Regina's legs, she leaned over her as she thrust in with the dildo.

"Oh...oh." Regina gasped as she lifted her hips to meet Anuli's thrusts. Soon, their hips were slapping together, their bodies sliding over each other as sweat slicked their skins.

Pleasure zinged through Anuli. She found that she loved being in charge of someone else's pleasure like this. The rapt expression on Regina's face with her lowered lids, glazed eyes, and a slightly opened mouth showed the woman was rushing towards another orgasm.

So was Anuli. Her body curled tight as she deepened the thrusts.

"Ah," they both cried as wave after wave of pleasure hit her, her body trembling.

She slumped on the bed beside Regina, panting.

Regina rolled to her side and placed her hand over Anuli's breast in what seemed like a possessive gesture.

A memory returned—of Uncle Joe doing the same thing after he'd had his way with her.

Anuli stiffened and sat up, pushing off the bed.

"What's the matter?" Regina sounded concerned.

The girl had no business being concerned about her. She didn't want her getting attached, especially since Regina was on the rebound from a broken relationship.

Anuli couldn't let anyone close to her again. Not Regina. Not anyone. She'd been through the heartache of losing Tessa to Peter. She wouldn't put herself through the pain again.

Taking a deep breath, she forced a smile on her face. "It's nothing. I just want a cigarette."

She grabbed the pack and lighter from her purse on the table.

"I'll have one then." Regina extended her hand, and Anuli gave her a stick before taking one for herself. She grabbed the ashtray and got back into bed.

The two of them smoked silently, Anuli engrossed in her thoughts as she made plans.

She was going to find Uncle Joe and lay his ghost to rest. Permanently.

Chapter Two

Tope killed the engine of his 2007 Toyota Prado after he stopped two houses across the street from where the blue and white coloured taxi had pulled up. His headlamps dimmed, the only light in the night coming from the other car.

Many people assumed that because he drove an SUV, that meant he was now rich and had money to burn. They would be wrong.

Sure, his job as Chief of Security for Park Hotels, Ltd meant that he earned enough money to be comfortable. But the car was a company car and he used it because it was practical. He travelled a lot across all the different sites where the hotel chain was located. He needed an all-weather, all-terrain vehicle to traverse the different landscapes he encountered on his journeys whether they were potholes on city roads or flooded gulley in country roads.

Now he sat in the darkened car watching the girl in the black mini-skirt and silver tank top stumble out of the cab first followed by Anuli in her tiger-striped stretch dress.

He'd seen them by chance at the bar where he'd gone to meet an old friend. He'd brushed past Anuli on his way out, recognising her instantly, although he hadn't seen her for a few weeks.

The first time he'd met Anuli, she'd been assigned to work in housekeeping as part of an employment contract she signed with one of the hotel owners where Tope worked.

From the day he'd seen her standing in Peter Oranye's penthouse suite, her brown eyes flashing with fiery fury at having been reassigned to a menial task, he hadn't been able to keep her out of his mind.

Anuli had long, layered, straightened brunette hair just past her shoulders, nutmeg skin tone, all on a medium height curvy body. He guessed she was somewhere in her mid-twenties.

When he noticed she hadn't been at work for a few days, he'd enquired about her absence and had been informed she'd been away due to upcoming exams at University. He'd been curious about her and had tried to find out as much about her as was possible. He'd even visited her university campus a few times as part of his investigations.

He'd found out that she had lived with Tessa Obum who was now engaged to Peter Oranye and had moved out of the shared digs.

Anuli loved hip hop music and would get up and dance in a club, sometimes rapping along. She didn't go to church, at least not on Sundays. He'd checked.

Anuli was spontaneous and careless as was proven when she suddenly shoved the other girl against the wall and started kissing her. It was a quiet cul-de-sac and the building was at the end.

The taxi had driven off and the security light inside the compound only illuminated them hazily. Still, they were outside and putting on a show for anyone in the vicinity to see.

His cock hardened, aching in his trousers as he watched Anuli part the girl's thighs with her right knee and squeeze her tit through her top. The girl arched her body as if wanting more.

Tope stifled a groan as he palmed his swollen dick through the fabric. Any heterosexual man who claimed he didn't get turned on from watching two women make out was lying to himself.

He was a voyeur. Nothing wrong with that. Especially if the people exhibiting were doing so willingly. Anuli and her lover had to know that it was possible for others to see them. So no harm in him sitting here and enjoying the show.

But he wanted to do more than watch. He'd watched her for a while already. He'd followed them discreetly as they'd left the bar and flagged down a taxi. He'd stayed behind the cab wanting to know which direction they were headed. When it became obvious they were going to Anuli's house, he'd slowed down, giving the cab space so it wasn't obvious he was following the car.

The girls separated just as the black side gate opened and a short man of medium build in a blue shirt and black trousers let them inside.

Seconds after Anuli and her friend disappeared behind the closed gate, Tope sat in the car, willing his hard-on to go down. There was no point punishing himself. He would have Anuli soon, especially if she carried on defying the contract she'd signed. Peter had already given his authorisation for Tope to deal with it as he saw fit.

Tope had a plan to bring Anuli to heel and he couldn't wait to get started. But first, he had a business trip to Calabar to get out of the way. There was a new Park Hotel opening up in the city. He'd recruited the security manager and staff. Now he just needed to finalise the rest of protection details and make sure everything was on track for the launch.

The week away would give Anuli the grace to get back to work. If she hadn't done so by the time he got back, then her ass would truly be his.

With a slow smile curling his lips, he started the car engine, did a three-point turn and drove home.

***

A week later, Anuli sat on a chair on the veranda of her studio, cigarette in one hand, puffing out smoke when her phone rang.

A smile curled her lips and her heart rate picked up speed when she saw the caller ID. She grabbed her phone from the top of the white plastic table next to her and brought it to her ear as she answered.

"Hi, babe," she said in the usual greeting she used with Tessa.

Regina who sat on the other side of the table furrowed her brows in a frown.

Anuli ignored her and diverted her gaze to the clothes line in the corner that had different coloured fabrics gently fluttering in the wind.

"Hey, Nuli. How are you?" Tessa sounded excited, her voice raised.

"I'm doing great, babes." Tessa would always be her girl, even if she was now living in a different city and betrothed to someone else. "How are you doing?"

"Fantastic. You won't believe where I am."

"Where?"

"In Peter's parents' house. Mehn, you should see it. It's huge. A mansion."

"Wow."

"But that's not the best thing."

"What is?"

"Peter's family. They are totally awesome. You know. Like really nice. I met them last weekend at the wedding. I told you, right."

"Yeah."

"So because Peter proposed to me last weekend, they invited me over to theirs to meet me properly. His mother has been fussing over me so much. You'd think I was a princess or something. His parents are so happy that Peter finally fell in love with another woman. His sister told me how devastated he was when his late girlfriend died. He'd been avoiding women so much they thought he'd never get married again."

"Wow."

"I know, right. So as far as they're concerned, I could be the messiah."

Anuli chuckled. "Seriously?"

"Yes. His mother is talking wedding bells already and making plans. I've hardly had time to wrap my mind around being engaged as it is. His father mentioned going to meet my family to make arrangements for wine-carrying ceremony and I nearly panicked."

"These people don't mess around."

"Are you telling me? I had to pull Peter aside in my panic about the igbankwu thing with family. So he's going to smooth the whole thing over with his father and explain that I don't really have a family for a traditional marriage. We're going to stick with the church wedding."

"Well, that's amazing. I'm so happy for you, babe. You deserve to be happy and I'm glad that Peter is doing all he can to make you happy."

"I know. Peter is totally awesome. I don't know what I did to earn someone like him."

"You totally deserve this after everything that's happened," Anuli said in a sober tone, a lump forming in her throat.

"I know. But I also want you to be this happy. I miss you, Nuli."

"I miss you too, babe."

"Why don't you come up to Enugu next week? You're not working during week days and I'm sure you can get some time off, if you ask Christopher. I can put in a good word for you."

"Erm, there's no need to do that," Anuli said a little too quickly. She didn't want to tell her friend that she hadn't been to work for a few weeks, since Tessa went to Enugu. Or that she hadn't been in touch with the manager of Park Hotel. Tessa would only start fussing if she knew Anuli hadn't been to work there for a while.

"Oh, okay. Are you going to speak to Christopher and come up then?" Tessa asked.

"Sorry, babe. But I have plans for next week."

"Is it work? Are you doing more hours at the hotel?"

"No, it's not that."

"You're still going to work at the hotel, aren't you?" Tessa asked.

Anuli hesitated. She didn't want to upset Tessa. On the other hand, she didn't want to blatantly lie to her friend. They'd shared so much and telling lies wasn't a part of it.

"Anuli?" Tessa probed.

"No. I haven't been to work in a few weeks," she finally confessed. This wasn't worth lying to her friend.

"What? A few weeks? Anuli, why now? Peter paid you a lot of money and you're not doing anything to earn it."

"You know I don't like that job. Cleaning hotel rooms wasn't what I signed up for."

"Maybe it wasn't. But you kept the two hundred and fifty grand he paid you. Are you going to pay it back?"

Anuli grimaced and got off the chair. She walked down the step and turned the corner, heading out of sight so Regina wouldn't hear what she said. She couldn't give back the money because she needed it for the plans she'd made concerning Uncle Joe.

She lowered her voice. "I can't afford to give it back. Look, I'll go back to work. Okay? There are just some things I need to deal with for a few weeks and then I'll go back."

"You promise?"

"I promise."

"Okay." Tessa puffed out a sigh. "What exactly are you dealing with? Did something happen? Do you need me to come down to Port Harcourt? I can be there in a day or so. I'm sure Peter won't mind."

"No. No. It's nothing for you to worry about. Nothing I can't take care of by myself." She just couldn't tell Tessa what she had planned. Uncle Joe was Anuli's problem not Tessa's. And the girl would only worry unnecessarily. Or even try to persuade her not to go through with it. But Anuli had made up her mind.

"Nuli, you know I don't like you hiding things from me—"

"Look, you have a new life now. Concentrate on Peter. Okay. I'll be fine. Haven't I always gotten through whatever life threw at me?"

"You have," Tessa said in a resigned voice.

"Then trust me now. I'll tell you when there's something to tell." She'd wait until she'd accomplished her goal before she told her friend.

"Okay—" There was the sound of someone talking in the background before Tessa added, "I have to go. Take care of yourself, Nuli."

"I will and you too. Bye." She pressed the end button and turned around only to find Regina standing a few steps away.

The girl had obviously followed her and from the sullen expression on her face, wasn't altogether pleased.

"Who was that?" Regina asked as she crossed her arms over her chest.

Anuli looked at her phone. "That was Tessa."

Kiru Taye

"You're still in touch with your ex? I thought you said she was engaged." Regina raised her voice a tad.

Anuli shook her head. She wasn't in the mood for a jealous lover. "Yes, Tessa is my ex. But she is also my best friend. That's not going to change because she's engaged to someone else."

She walked past Regina, back up the step and into the chair she'd vacated. Regina followed back to her seat.

Awkward silence settled between them for a few minutes. Anuli's neighbours were all at work or out, so they didn't have anyone to disturb them.

The phone call from Tessa made warmth bloom across her chest. A smile tugged at her lips as she remembered how excited Tessa had been about being fussed over by her future in-laws.

"My ex and I are not friends. I'm not in touch with her." Regina broke the silence.

Anuli sighed and tapped her cigarette tip on the tray, dislodging the ash. "I understand but if you were to keep in touch, I won't mind."

Regina reared back. "Really? So you don't mind if I see other people?"

Anuli shrugged. Like in any relationship, people got attached once sex was involved. It was no different from Regina. They had been spending more time together since the other night when they'd had sex for the first time. Regina seemed to be here every day.

Anuli hadn't minded but it was now time to sever the ties. She couldn't have the girl around for what was to come.

"I don't mind if you see other people. In fact, I think it's probably best if you do. I'm not ready for a serious relationship. And you're also dealing with your broken relationship. You need time to get over it."

Regina opened her mouth to say something but Anuli cut her off.

"Before you say anything, think about it. Do you really want to get tied down again so soon?"

The girl puffed a long breath. "You're right. I'd rather wait. But you know it's so tough finding women who are like us. There's so much hatred and prejudice out there. So when I meet someone who returns my affections in any way, I want to cling on to them."

Anuli nodded. This was Nigeria where being homosexual was considered taboo and practically illegal by association. Same-sex relationships couldn't be displayed publicly and gay clubs were banned. So it was difficult to identify other same-sex lovers. She'd only found out about Regina and her ex through the grapevine on campus.

"I understand. But I'm really not in the frame of mind for anything more. You understand, right?"

"I do."

"Good." Anuli stood and gathered her things. "Come on. There's somewhere I need to get to this afternoon."

Chapter Three

Later that afternoon, Anuli dropped Regina off at her house. The girl still lived with her parents in a middle class suburb, a two-level semi-detached house on a quiet street.

Regina's parents didn't know she was a lesbian. It wasn't the kind of thing you could easily tell your African parents. Although Regina's father was a doctor and her mother worked for an oil company which proved they were educated enough to be enlightened, it wasn't any less daunting to come out to them. Anuli was glad she didn't have any living relatives she had to worry about in that sense.

"Can I come over tomorrow?" Regina asked as she got out of the taxi which had stopped outside the gated entrance. She leaned against the open window.

"No." Anuli didn't bother getting out of the car. She needed it to drop her where she was going. "I'm going to be out of town for a few days, so it's best not to come over. I'll call you when I get back."

"Okay. I'll look forward to it." She blew a kiss.

Anuli stroked the bare skin of Regina' arm and blew a kiss back. "Take care of yourself."

"Bye." Regina waved.

"Bye." Her chest tightened. She didn't think she'd call Regina when she got back. She straightened, plastered a smile on her face and told the driver where to head. She gave a wave to Regina before the girl walked into the compound.

Anuli relaxed back into the seat, her mind churning with the thought of what was to come. She'd spent the last week making the necessary arrangements and finding out as much as she could.

Peter had already been investigating Uncle Joe and Tessa's father's activities. They'd found out Tessa's father was still alive, although the injury he'd sustained had left him a wheelchair user.

Tessa didn't want anything to do with the man, which Anuli could understand. But Anuli wasn't so willing to forgive the men what they had done.

The investigations underway should ensure the men were eventually prosecuted. But Anuli wouldn't kid herself. Men like Uncle Joe didn't go to jail, especially since he was now a high-ranking member of the Nigerian Police Force.

When they reached the area, she told the driver to stop and paid him. Then she got out of the car. She would have to walk the rest of the way.

The sun was low in the sky as she strode down a sandy, unpaved street with gullies. It was a warm day but the temperature wasn't too high as it had rained earlier. Bare-chested kids played on street and women in makeshift kiosks sold wares on small tables. There was a woman roasting fish and plantains on an open fire and customers stood waiting for the food. She stopped to ask one of the women for directions and she pointed it out to her.

Anuli's neck prickled as if she was being watched. She glanced back but didn't see anything out of the ordinary. She supposed the people on the street were staring at her because she was a stranger here. Nothing extraordinary there.

She reached a single-level house that was set close to the road and had a provision shop on one side.

"Good evening," she greeted a young girl with cornrow plaits in her hair and who sat on a white plastic outside the shop. "I dey look for Bosco. Na here be the place?"

She had to speak in the local street language otherwise she would stand out.

The girl looked her up and down with curious eyes. "Good evening, aunty. You want Bosco?"

"Eh, Na him."

"Na this be the place. Just enter for there. Na the second door for your right." She pointed to the open communal entryway.

"Thank you." Anuli glanced behind before walking into the shadowed corridor illuminated only by the sun rays coming from both ends. Six painted wooden doors stationed at regular intervals on parallel sides led to different residences. She knocked on the second green wooden door.

A tall, dark-skinned man with a scar running down the side of his face loomed on the other side of the open threshold.

Her heart jolted. She hadn't heard footsteps or even a squeak of the hinges as the door unlocked. Surprising, as the walls in these types of buildings

were notoriously thin and the premises looked old
enough for the doors to creak.

She swallowed to clear the lump in her throat.
"Bosco?"

His bleary amber eyes indicated he may have
just woken from sleep. He wore a pair of khaki
shorts only, dark, tattooed, honed muscles on
display.

"Na me." His voice was deep and rough. He
nodded as he sized her up, making tingles skitter
over her skin.

He reminded her of another man. Tope. Her
breath hitched. She'd always had a thing for big,
tough-looking men.

"My name na Anuli. Mike Ocha send me come
here."

"Mike Ocha?"

She nodded, keeping her shoulders back and chin
high. This man was dangerous. She didn't doubt it.
And she couldn't show any fear. Otherwise, he
would take advantage. "He tell me say you get
wetin I dey find."

"No wahala. Make you enter." He moved out of
the way.

She sashayed into the one-bed apartment that
comprised of a low bed in the corner, a small black
leather sofa at another end with a large TV
mounted on the egg-shell wall. There was also a
small coffee table and a wardrobe made from light
wood and a small kitchenette situated at the far
end.

She stood by the sofa, not wanting to sit down
without his invitation.

He watched her, projecting deadly silence before he smiled, showing white teeth. "Oya, siddon for that chair. Tell me wetin you want."

Her hands turned clammy and she brushed them against her jeans trousers and sat on the sofa with a squish of foam. She cleared her throat.

"I need a gun," she blurted out.

He didn't flinch or show any outward sign that her request startled her. She supposed he probably got the request frequently if he was a weapons dealer.

He settled in the single armchair. "Wetin you wan use am do?"

She frowned. It wasn't his business. "Does it matter? Look, I bring money." She reached into her bag and pulled out the brown envelope with the cash she'd taken from the bank earlier.

The smart phone on the coffee table buzzed and flashed. He didn't say anything as he leaned forward and picked it up.

Anuli raised her eyebrows and crossed her arms over her chest as she watched him flick the screen of the gadget, read the message and then type out something.

She'd offering cash for an item which he obviously sold, and yet he didn't seem in a hurry to make a deal. Was it because she was a woman? She couldn't be the first woman to come here seeking a weapon.

"Am I the first woman to buy a gun from you?" she asked, reverting to classroom English in irritation. If he didn't want her money, she'd find someone else. The only problem being that her time remained short and she needed the gun today.

He lifted his gaze slowly, nonchalantly, amber eyes pinning her in place.

"You're not my first," he spoke in English that made her breath catch both from its perfection as well as its innuendo. He gave her body that lazy sweep again that made her pulse pound and her panties wet.

"You..." She shook her head and licked her lips, unable to form words as her heart raced.

He gave her that smile again, full of white teeth that reminded her of a shark. A deadly predator. "You think you're the only one who can speak English?"

She swallowed. She wasn't judgemental. It was just that he surprised her. She looked around the space and back at him, trying not to squirm.

"No. I wasn't trying to be snobby. It's just that with what I heard about you, I didn't expect..." she trailed off again.

He still hadn't covered up. His casual attitude made him appear like a street thug. But his piercing eyes held the intelligence of a man who seemed to be more than he projected.

"Yes, I'm a University graduate and a gun runner. This is Nigeria and we have to do what we do to survive." He shrugged and picked up his buzzing phone again.

Relaxing into the sofa, she stared at him, curious about his story, her interest in him peaking.

Men like Bosco fascinated her, called to the woman in her, their masculinity defined by the knife-edged danger they oozed. The clean-cut Peters of the world didn't appeal to her emotionally. Men with silver spoons in their mouths weren't her thing. She wanted a man who could relate to her back story. Men with darkness inside them. Men like Tope.

What the hell? Why did that man's name enter her head again? She was thinking about Bosco, wasn't she?

But it was the image of Tope back in her mind again. She shoved it aside and gritted her teeth. "So are you going to sell me the gun or do I have to go somewhere else?"

"Of course." He stood up and walked over to the wardrobe and came back with a black leather bag which he dropped on the low table. Unzipping it, he pulled out a stainless steel gun.

"This is a Colt semi automatic with an eight round magazine." He pulled back the top and it clicked. Then he placed it on the table. "It's one hundred grand."

"One hundred? I only brought eighty. Will that do?"

He shook his head. "That gun is over two hundred thousand naira. I'm giving it to you for less than half price already."

Her palms sweated and she swiped them on her jeans again. She could go and bring more money but she wanted to leave here with the gun. Wasn't sure if he would even sell to her if she walked out now.

He met her gaze, holding it. He relaxed into his seat, legs spread apart, showing a tent in his shorts.

Heat flared in her veins as her heart beats strengthened. Mutual attraction sizzled in the air between them. Perhaps he would take the rest of the money in kind. She hadn't accepted payment for sex in weeks. In this case, she would be paying with sex. But she didn't mind. She missed the hardness of a man.

She licked her lips, tasting her cherry lip-gloss, and shifted forward in her chair. "What if I made up the balance in kind?"

His eyes brightened with interest. "What do you have in mind?"

She flicked her gaze from him to the bed. "What if I let you fuck me to cover the balance?"

He leaned back into his chair. "You really want this gun that badly?"

"I do. I can't leave here today without it. What do you say?"

He smiled at her again. "I say okay. But you don't go until I say I'm done."

"And you don't enter my body without protection."

"Fair enough."

Her pulse thumped as she exhaled in relief. "Okay. First, show me how to use the gun."

"No wahala." He leaned forward, picked up the weapon and showed her how to remove and load the magazine and how to release the safety catch.

Then he stood behind her, placed the gun in her right hand and showed her how to sight and take aim. She used her left hand to balance the weight of the gun and to stop it from shaking.

She sucked in a deep breath. Bosco's masculine musk filled her nostrils just as his heat stroked her back, although the only place they made contact was his rough, large hand on hers. Her body trembled with want.

A knock sounded on the door.

"Hold on," Bosco said as he stepped away.

Anuli shoved the weapon into her bag and left the envelope with the cash on the table.

Bosco opened the door. "Come in," he said to the visitor.

Anuli couldn't see the person as she was seated behind the open slab. But she wondered who it was that Bosco invited in, considering they were supposed to have sex to settle the balance for the gun.

Her mouth dropped open when the hulk of a man loomed over her, his thunderous expression instantly recognisable.

Tope! What the hell was he doing here?

Chapter Four

Anuli's sharp gasp was audible enough for everyone in the room to hear it. Heart racing, she struggled to breathe properly, which made her feel light-headed.

How did Tope suddenly turn up at the place she'd gone to buy a gun?

She pulled her bag against her chest and squeezed her eyes shut. Maybe she was hallucinating or something.

"What are you doing here?" Tope's deep voice had her eyelids flying open.

"I—I should be asking you that." Her voice sounded soft and shaky. Why the hell did she turn into a quivering mass whenever he was around? Now her primary mental response was to find somewhere to hide so he wouldn't discover the exact reason she'd come here. Why the hell did she have to hide, damn him? She'd arrived here first. He had no business being here. "In fact, I think you should leave as I have business to conclude with Bosco."

The man in question shut the door and went to sit on the bed in the corner as if this wasn't his apartment and he didn't have anything to do with what was going on.

"Is that so?" Tope crossed his arms over his chest, his feet planted apart, drawing her attention to the bulging muscles of his arms that stretched his T-shirt as well as the ones on his sturdy thighs encased in blue denim. "Well, Bosco knows better than to do *business* with my woman without my permission."

"Your woman?" She bolted upright, standing to her full five feet five in the three-inch platform shoes, eyes glaring at him. "I'm not your woman!"

They'd barely said two words to each other since she'd met him months ago aside from the very brief conversation they'd had at the bar last week. She was certainly not his anything.

He dropped his arms, taking a step in her direction. This close, he was so broad, so tall, he seemed to occupy all the room. All her focus was on him, his dark gaze, his hard features, and his unyielding posture. The air in the room constricted along with the space. She felt claustrophobic and breathless.

"Last weekend, I warned you that if you didn't go back to work, your ass would be mine. You didn't go back to work. This means you were inviting me to own your ass." He lowered his head so they were at eye level. "Well, Tiger. Your ass now belongs to me, which makes you my woman."

What was with him calling her Tiger? He'd used that word last weekend as well. She remembered that she'd been wearing a tiger-striped dress when she'd last seen him. Warmth bloomed across her chest. He'd given her a pet name. So sweet. Not!

She stiffened her stance and rolled her eyes. "Well, oga sir. I never gave you permission to claim my anything. Anyway, my best friend is engaged to the owner of Park Hotel. I have permission not to be there. I can report you for harassment."

It was a blatant lie but he couldn't know, right?

"In that case, you should call your friend and tell her where you are and how I'm harassing you. Or even better, call Peter directly and report me." He strode over to the armchair and sank into it, his body taking up all the space.

She stared at him with narrowed eyes. This man wasn't budging. He was going to call her bluff. She couldn't call Tessa, let alone report him to Peter. Damn him.

"If you're not leaving, then that's your business but I'm going to complete my deal with Bosco."

He turned his attention to Bosco. "What are you selling her?"

She swivelled to Bosco. "Don't tell him!"

He ignored her request. "A Colt 45 semi."

Anuli growled in frustration and clenched her hands into fists.

Tope sucked in air through his teeth. "This my woman na hard babe. How much she give you?"

"Eighty. But she say she go settle the balance."

The two men continued the conversation as if she wasn't in the room with them.

"Hello! I'm right here. You can't talk about me as if I'm not here." She stomped her foot.

Tope tilted his head to the side and looked at her. "So how are you planning on completing the payment for the gun?"

"It's none of your business," she snapped.

"I think we've already established that it is my business. You are my woman. The sooner you accept it, the sooner we move on."

"I'm not your woman, damn you."

"If you say so," he said in a mocking tone that made it seem she was protesting too much.

Even Bosco didn't seem to believe her claim if the smirk on his face was anything to go by. What was it with men anyway?

"Mr Bosco, how are we going to do this? Maybe I should bring your balance tomorrow." She clutched her purse to her side.

"That's not what we agreed. It's payment on delivery." He grinned at her.

"You want to collect the balance now?" Her voice rang with shock.

"Of course. That's what we agreed. Otherwise, you leave the gun and come back when you're ready to pay the full price. Mind you, the price might go up next time." He winked at her.

He was blackmailing her. Damn him. Damn Tope. Did they plan this? How was that possible?

She turned her glare on Tope, dropping her bag on the sofa. "You do realise that I'm supposed to pay him in kind. Through sex."

"That's one option. Or you could admit that you're my woman. And I'll pay the balance for you."

"Are you fucking deaf? I'm not your woman. Get over it." The whole thing was beginning to irritate her.

"In that case, get on the bed and let Bosco fuck you." He pointed at the divan.

She raised one brow, hands akimbo. "And you're just going to sit there?"

"Yes. It shouldn't matter. You say you're not mine and Bosco invited me to be here. So go ahead." He waved his hand as if urging her on. "I like watching anyway."

Something unfurled low in her belly at his words. He was a voyeur. She was an exhibitionist. Seemed like a match made in heaven, right?

She shook her head. Would he really look on while she took another man inside her? Was this guy for real?

He didn't appear upset. His head tilted to the side and he had a slow smile building on his face, as if he wanted to know what she'd do next.

Shit. Her heart raced. Adrenaline rushing in her veins. Heat flushed her skin. Anger morphed to excitement and desire.

She glanced from Tope to Bosco. Both men watched her, wearing almost identical expressions of curiosity.

Tope relaxed back in the chair, his legs spread out, and a bulge obvious in his jeans. Bosco lay across the bed on his back, sporting a tent in his shorts. He didn't seem fazed that someone would watch them too.

"Can I ask something?" She directed her question to Tope.

"Yeah?" His expression turned unreadable as if he shielded himself from her words.

"Do you two know each other? I mean I know you know each other because he let you in without a discussion and you obviously knew I was here. But are you friends or something?"

A grin spread on Tope's face. Bosco chuckled.

"Yes. You can say we're friends." Tope glanced at Bosco and they communicated silently, which they'd been doing since he'd walked into the room.

Just her luck that the gun dealer she picked had to be a friend of Tope.

"What?" she asked.

"We're waiting for you. Or you can admit the obvious. But you're not going to, so we're waiting."

"Right." Licking her lower lip, she gave them both another quick glance. Her heart thumped hard against her chest as she tugged the hem of her tank top and pulled it over her head.

Warmth flooded her body. She got a kick out of putting her body on display. Got turned on when men watched her and she knew they wanted her in the most physically intimate ways possible. This scene could've been one of her fantasies being played out in real life.

She unhooked her bra as she became aware of the strong beats of her heart, thumping hard and loud.

Somebody sighed in appreciation when she tossed her bra on the sofa. Was that Tope or Bosco? Movement from Bosco showed he'd shifted to the end of the bed, the wood creaking a little.

A glance at Tope had him watching her with interested, hooded eyes. He didn't look like a man who was about to kill his friend for staring at someone he'd labelled 'his woman' taking her clothes off.

This was really going to happen.

She moistened her lips with her tongue as she unclasped her jeans and shoved them down her thighs, hooking her fingers into the sides of her panties and pushing them off together.

Bosco gave a low whistle. He got full view of her rounded bum as she bent over to tug the jeans off with her shoes.

Her pussy clenched tight, heart rate skyrocketing.

She'd done this enough times it seemed like a routine, stripping in front of men.

Yet this time stood different. Tope's penetrating stare scorched her bare flesh, making her hand tremble as she placed her clothes on the sofa and reached into her bag to take out the condom foil.

Bosco didn't move from his position on the bed. Neither did he take his shorts off. He glanced at Tope who gave a nod as if he gave permission. Bosco raised himself on his elbows before standing up.

It hit her then.

Tope was in control of the situation. Bosco wouldn't touch her without Tope's consent. It didn't matter that Bosco wanted to fuck her anyway or that she'd denied being Tope's woman. The connection between the two men was stronger than the sexual desire burning in the air.

Damn these men!

Her body tensed as some of her earlier fury returned. She would prove to Tope that he couldn't intimidate her.

She ambled over to the bed and shoved Bosco's chest. Not fighting, he bounced on the mattress covered with sky blue cotton sheets. She tugged down his shorts down and set his dark, hard bobbing cock free.

He smiled at her as she ripped the condom open and rolled it down his length and groaned when she wrapped her hand around him, stroking him gently.

She settled on her knees on the floor and took his cock into her mouth, tasting the apple flavour of the condom. She worked him with her tongue and hand, making sure to nuzzle his perineum and balls. He smelled of sweat and man, no cologne to mask his scent. He groaned and jerked his hips in rhythm.

His response excited her, her pussy pulsing in tune with her heartbeats. A glance in Tope's direction showed him sitting with a glazed expression, his palm stroking his cock through his jeans.

Heat flushed her skin, tingles spreading. Her core clenched, clamping around nothing. She needed a man's hardness filling and stroking her. She withdrew her mouth from Bosco's dick. He came out with a pop.

She climbed onto his lap and slowly slid her pussy over his sheathed cock.

"Ohhhh." She moaned as she took him deep inside her, rolling her hips as pleasure zinged through her.

She set the pace, gliding up and down slowly. He felt good. So good.

Bosco didn't take over. Neither did he touch her body, except for where they were joined. He allowed her to use his body as if he was a toy for her delight.

"You can touch me, you know," she said in a breathless voice as she pushed off with her hands on his chest and slid down on him. She did all the work. While she enjoyed taking charge, it wasn't the best sensation she could have. She needed someone's hands on her too. She needed to be held and stroked externally as well as internally.

Bosco grinned at her in the sexy lopsided way that sent her heart racing. But he didn't move his hands from where they gripped the other side of the bed tightly, the muscles straining. As if he fought himself not to touch her. Was he waiting for Tope's permission?

Damn him. Damn both of them. She could touch herself. If she pinched her nipple hard enough, she could have an orgasm. She lifted her hands but before she could reach her breasts, someone gripped her upper arms and tugged back.

She tilted her head to see Tope standing behind her, restraining her limbs.

"What are you doing?" she asked, a little disorientated in a haze of lust.

"This fucking is not about your pleasure. This is payment for him. So he gets the pleasure," Tope whispered close to her right ear. "You don't get an orgasm unless I allow you to have one. Whether you like it or not, your body is now mine. You don't get to have sex, masturbate or climax without my approval."

As Tope spoke, Bosco started thrusting upward into her pussy, melting her brain even further as pleasure rose.

"What?" she asked. She couldn't understand what he was saying. All she knew was that her body thrilled, hovering over the cliff of climax. But she just couldn't seem to tumble over.

"You heard me, Tiger. Beg me for your pleasure. Beg me to let Bosco fuck your little kitty until you come."

His low whisper in her ear drove her insane, and coupled with having Bosco inside her, she had no chance of resisting his words. "Please...I want to come."

"That's my girl. Bosco, you heard her," Tope said as he twisted her arms at the back so that her head turned to him.

Then his mouth descended on her, devouring her lips, claiming her in a way no man had done before. She didn't kiss clients, hadn't kissed a man in years. She tried to push him off but got distracted. A hand squeezed her left breast while another parted her labia, stroking her clit.

"Oh...oh." She melted. She tingled as if she was being stroked all over, hands everywhere. Her body heated, writhed. Her breaths quickened. Nothing before now had felt this good. The combination of being restrained and being caressed by so many hands made a tsunami of pleasure surge through her. She soared.

"Tope!" Her orgasm detonated like she'd never had it before, sending her body shaking so much, tears streaked down her face.

Tope broke the kiss and stroked her face with callused fingers. "I've got you. I've always got you."

He cradled her even though she still sat on top of Bosco who had stopped moving. Had Bosco climaxed too? His cock still throbbed hard and hot inside her.

In answer to her silent question, Bosco lifted her off his body and onto Tope's lap as he now sat on the bed.

"Bosco, where are you going? You're still hard," she protested, reaching out, trying to get him to stay.

"Don't worry about me," Bosco replied, getting off the mattress. "I'll take care of myself."

He removed the condom, pulled on the shorts and left the room.

It took a few seconds for her brain to engage after the mind-melting orgasm. What the hell just happened? What was she doing?

First of all, she'd allowed Tope to kiss her, although technically 'allow' wasn't the word. He'd taken the kiss from her, fiercely, almost brutally and she'd been unable to stop her body from responding to the power of his embrace.

And another thing, she didn't cuddle after sex. So why was she letting Tope hold her in his arms as if she belonged here? She sighed with pleasure, her body warm and replete. She wanted to close her eyes and bask in his heat and strength. In his safety.

She couldn't stay here. He thought she was his woman but she wouldn't accept it. Couldn't accept it. She belonged to no one. Never again.

What she'd said while she'd been lost in a fog of lust didn't matter. She could plead insanity. She would've been insane for allowing him to take over.

And what was with Bosco not coming? She was supposed to pay the man with sex. What was the point if he didn't climax?

Angrily, she shoved at Tope's chest. He let her go. Her legs wobbled a little as they hit the hard linoleum floor. She stiffened and grabbed her clothes, putting them back on with jerky motions.

Tope didn't say anything as he watched her get dressed. She didn't look at him. Didn't want to see the expression on his face. He probably gloated because he'd gotten his way.

She grabbed her bag. The cash bundle was on the table and she'd put the gun in her bag earlier. So she assumed it was still there but didn't check. She got what she came for so there was no more reason to stay here. She headed for the door.

"Where do you think you're going?" Tope's voice was low and rough.

"Where else? Home. I'm done here," she snapped.

"Not without me." His tone was matter of fact, as if it were a foregone conclusion.

She swivelled around. "Look. I don't know what's going on with you. Whether you're turning into a stalker or what. But I don't need you following me. I can get home by myself."

Before she could reach the door, she was hauled off the floor, over his shoulder, her bum up in the air and her head hanging down his back.

"What the—"

His palm landed on her bum in successive hard swats, shutting her up and making her stifle a sob. Shit. At first, she struggled, kicked out. His grip around her thighs only clamped tight. He kept spanking her, each smack jolting her body against his, increasing their physical contact. A switch flicked in her brain, letting in a flicker of light into her dark world. Her ass blazed even as wet heat dripped from her pussy. She slumped against him in silence, panting to catch her breath as peace settled on her mind.

"Now, are you going to behave yourself?" he asked, his tone stern and unforgiving.

She'd done some bad things. But no one had ever spoken to her in such a manner. People tended to back off rather than confront her. Surprisingly, the serious, almost old-fashioned way he spoke had a soothing effect.

"Yes," she said in a sullen voice, feeling like a ten-year-old who'd been chastised.

"Good, because you're coming home with me."

Chapter Five

Tope gripped Anuli's thighs with his left arm, holding her in place as she sank over his left shoulder. His right hand caressed her bum which he'd just spanked. He groped the right cheek.

Her breath hitched as she tensed.

He soothed the sting with his palm.

She sighed, sagging again.

He carried on massaging her soft flesh down to the back of her knees and back up.

She mewled like a kitten. She loved having him touch her, even if she wouldn't admit it.

Oh, she was a kitten even though sometimes she acted like a wild cat. This was the reason he'd nicknamed her Tiger. She had the ability to be tame in his arms. Yet she could shred him with her claws if he didn't handle her with care.

She'd proven it earlier by having sex with his friend in his presence without any fear of his reaction.

Of course, he'd allowed it. He could've dragged her out of here kicking and screaming.

But he was learning her and he'd wanted to find out what kind of person she was. She'd shown him and he would never underestimate her.

She'd taken a shot at him today by having sex with Bosco, even if she didn't realise she'd been firing blanks.

He now knew that she was capable of shooting the gun she'd purchased at a target. He just didn't know who that was and why. But he'd find out.

Slowly, he lowered her onto her feet, sliding her body against his from chest to thighs so she could feel all of him, including the rock-hard erection pushing against his denim trousers.

Gripping her right arm, he pointed at the sofa. "Sit down."

Her face puckered, brows creasing. She didn't say anything as she lowered onto the seat. She winced sharply and adjusted her bum. She wouldn't be sitting comfortably for a while. The discomfort would remind her not to sass him in a hurry.

He suppressed a smile. "Stay there and wait for me. I need to speak to Bosco briefly and then we're heading to mine."

She frowned and opened her mouth. "I—"

"I swear to God, if you're not in that exact spot when I come back, I will spank your bottom so hard, you won't sit down for a week. And I will do it in public. Dare me if you want to find out how strict I am."

Her eyes widened and her frown deepened but she didn't say anything.

Good. He left her in the room and went outside. Bosco leaned against his SUV parked in front of the building, a small plastic bottle of water in his right hand and a brown paper parcel in his left hand.

The sun was low in the orange sky. A little breeze fluttered paper and plastic wrappers in a mini whirlwind that cooled the humid dusk air.

Bosco handed him the package and lifted the bottle of water to his lips.

Tope gripped the hardness of the metal gun inside. He clicked the lock for his car and pulled open the driver's door. He tugged the glove compartment, shoved the parcel inside and took out his cheque book and pen. Leaning against the seat, he filled it in for Twenty Thousand Naira made payable to Bosco and signed it.

Straightening, he handed the slip to his friend who took it.

"Thanks," Bosco said and after a few heartbeats added, "You're serious about this babe."

"You bet I am." Tope sat on the seat, his feet on the unpaved road beside the gutter covered with metal slabs. Around them, dusk was settling in. He smelled the roasting plantains from the stall across the street.

At the shop, just to the left, the shop girl packed small cans of tomato paste into a black plastic bag and took the cash handed by the female customer in long grey skirt and brown top. She handed over the bag of groceries as well as the woman's change before the woman thanked her and walked away.

"What are you going to do about the gun?" Bosco's voice drew his attention.

Tope had taken the weapon from Anuli's bag while she'd been distracted with having sex with Bosco. He'd made the decision to take it from her the second she'd started striping.

Any woman whom he'd already claimed as his who would boldly have sex with another man in his presence and not fear his repercussion would be bold enough to use the weapon on anyone. Since he didn't know her intention for buying the gun, he'd be stupid to leave it in her possession.

Anyway, he'd just given Bosco the balance of the money she owed, which meant she now owed him.

She thought sex had been payment for the gun. Instead, the sex had been Tope's way of learning about her, as well as a distraction so he could remove the gun from her bag.

He'd controlled the situation right from the start.

Right from the moment he'd found out she'd been looking for somewhere to buy a gun.

The discovery had been coincidental. He'd assigned Siki, a member of his security team, to watch her for the week he'd been away in Calabar. On Wednesday, Siki had called him to say that Anuli had been to see Mike Ocha. He'd know instantly that trouble was brewing. Mike was a small time crook and dealer.

Anuli risked her personal safety by interacting with such men. Not to mention whatever threat she perceived that would drive her to buy a weapon.

While Port Harcourt was big, as a security specialist, Tope had one foot in the local underworld. He knew the key players, if not by interaction, then by reputation. He needed to know who was who in order to do his job properly and keep his clients' properties and employees safe.

So when he'd contacted Mike Ocha and the man had told him that Anuli had been asking about where to buy a gun, Tope had intervened. Mike said that Anuli was supposed to come back at a later date to pick up the weapon.

Tope had instructed Mike to direct her to Bosco. He'd compensated the man for the loss of income. When Anuli had come back to collect the gun, the man had apologised and said he'd been unable to obtain what she'd asked for and sent her to Bosco instead.

Tope trusted Bosco and needed someone who would work with him to find out what Anuli was planning. He'd asked Bosco to stall her when she turned up.

"I'm going to keep the gun and find out why she needs it," Tope said. "If someone has threatened her, then they would have me to deal with."

"She didn't look like she's going to tell you anything," Bosco said.

Tope chuckled. "You're kidding. We're going to be spending a lot of time together in the next few days and weeks so she's going to learn that I don't give up."

His friend smiled. "Rather you than me. You picked a firecracker this time. She's going to keep you on your toes."

"About time someone did. I miss having a woman in my life." The casual affairs didn't count. He wasn't built to be alone. He yearned for companionship. But he needed a woman made of steel on the inside to cope with him and his life.

Anuli fit the bill. A little soft and rough on the exterior but hard at the core. She was his Ferrero Rocher—sweet and crunchy chocolate with a nut centre.

"I need her." His chest constricted at the admission. His friend met his gaze and nodded. They had a shared past, pleasurable as well as painful. The nod signified that Bosco understood how important Anuli was to Tope and would always have his back no matter what.

Puffing out air, he straightened and shut the door. "We're going to head off."

"Okay." Bosco turned and walked across the gangway, onto the terrace and into the corridor splitting the dwelling into two sides with apartment doors facing each other.

Tope followed him. When Bosco opened the door to his place, Tope walked in first only to stop short when he found Anuli lying across the sofa, eyes closed. The room was now dim, very little light coming in from the window as the sun disappeared from the horizon.

Bosco turned on a battery-powered lamp, filling the room with white light that made Anuli look fragile in sleep.

Tope's heart did a jerk in his chest seeing her so subdued. It was the first time he'd seen her open and looking so young. His chest tightened as he strode across and sat on the coffee table. Leaning across, he pushed some hair behind her ear and stroked her smooth cheek.

"Anuli, it's time to go," he said.

She jerked upright, her eyes flying open. "Sorry. I—I was just lying down to take the weight off my bum."

"It's okay," he said with a smile. "Come on. Let's go home."

He helped her stand but she shook his hand off.

"My gun. You took it. I want it back," she said, the frown back on her face.

She must have checked her bag and found the weapon gone. He was surprised she hadn't come outside to ask for it. Perhaps she'd been afraid he would spank her in public.

Good. At least she feared something.

"I've got the gun. You can have it later, if you behave yourself."

"It's my gun. I paid for it. You have no right to take it." She cocked her hip, hand akimbo.

He took a step towards her. "It seems your bum isn't sore enough and I need to tan it more."

Glaring at him, she backed up but didn't say anything.

He turned to Bosco. "Ol boy. We go see."

"Catch you later," his friend said with a grin.

"Let's go," Tope said to Anuli and headed for the door.

Outside Bosco's apartment, Tope waited for her and placed his arm across her stiff shoulders when she came out. They strode outside into the low light. He kept his arms around her so that anyone in the neighbourhood would know she belonged to him. She didn't appear altogether pleased but she didn't argue either. He opened the door and helped her into the car before walking around to get into the driver's seat.

She sat silently as he reversed, turned and headed back to the main road leading to his place.

Tope rolled the car forward, the beam of headlamps highlighting the column of cars crawling in the traffic. Although it was Saturday night, some Port Harcourt roads encountered the odd congestion especially if there'd been an incident. Luckily, he didn't have far to go before he reached his dwelling.

He glanced at the woman in the passenger seat beside him. The interior of the car remained dim, backlit by the reflection of the headlights bouncing off the car in front.

Anuli sat ramrod straight, facing the windscreen, making extra effort not to look at him. He smothered the slow grin forming. His skin had tingled a few times since they'd left Bosco's place so he could bet that she'd been snatching glances when he wasn't looking.

When they got to his neighbourhood, he stopped the car in front of a buka that he frequented. There was a power failure in the area and living alone, he rarely cooked at home especially since he travelled a lot.

"Let's get something to eat," he said as he killed the engine.

"I'm not hungry," she replied. "Why don't you just give me the gun and I'll take a taxi home."

"Well, I'm hungry and the only home you're going to tonight is mine. Come on or I'll carry you." He got out of the car.

She huffed and got out too. He grinned as he walked over to her side and took her hand.

The area was busy—pedestrians, cars, stalls lit with kerosene lamps. The noise of generators mixed with cars horns and conversations.

The makeshift single-level restaurant he frequented had a generator functioning so he was guaranteed to get a cool drink with the hot meal.

Fluorescent bulbs lit the place which was half full with customers. Rotating standing fans stood at different corners attempting to cool the air. Luckily, it wasn't a hot night.

"Oga Tope, welcome," the proprietor greeted as he strode in.

"Mama Ejima, good evening," he replied as she ushered them to a table which she usually reserved for him. He knew most of the people in the restaurant and waved or nodded in greeting as he walked by. He pulled out a chair for Anuli who sat down.

"This na iyawo mi," Tope continued, introducing Anuli in a tone that anyone around could hear. He was staking his claim openly. There was no point referring to her as a girlfriend. He hadn't cared about a woman as deeply as he cared for this one. He wasn't interested in a fling. "Her name na Anuli."

"Eyahhh! Oga Tope wife. So you marry Igbo girl." The woman beamed a big smile at him, then at Anuli. "I happy for una well well. My Igbo sister. Ahhh. Welcome, you hear? Oga Tope na good man ooh."

Anuli didn't say anything. She didn't even smile for the benefit of the woman who was being courteous. He made a note. It wasn't exactly being rude but she wasn't being respectful either. He would have to reprimand her for it.

Mama Ejima passed them the menus. "Make I bring your usual?"

"Eh, bring two glasses with the bottle. Me and my wife go share am." He gambled that Anuli wouldn't mind drinking Guinness.

"Okay. I dey come now now." The woman walked off.

Anuli leaned across the table and hissed in a low voice. "Why did you tell her I was your wife? I'm not."

He leaned forward and lowered his voice. "Do you think I'm kidding when I say you belong to me? You're in for a shock. This is my neighbourhood. My mother was born not far from here. I be indigene, son of the soil. Everybody in this restaurant knows me and now they know you are mine. They are my eyes and ears. If you do anything you're not supposed to and they see you, be sure that they will let me know. And I will set your ass ablaze."

Her mouth dropped open in shock.

Grinning, he winked at her. He loved seeing her surprised expression and he had a few more surprises in store for her.

Chapter Six

"And another thing," Tope continued in a low voice. "You better be nice to Mama Ejima. She was being pleasant to you earlier and you ignored her like a petulant child. Do it again and your bottom will feel the effect."

He leaned back into his seat and flashed white teeth in a grin.

Anuli bit back the 'fuck you' that rose to her tongue. She didn't have to be nice to anyone, especially since they were his friends. She didn't want to be here. She should've been on her way home, getting ready for a night out.

Instead, she ground her teeth as she bristled, body tense. She could so slap Tope's face right now. She curled her hands into fists, knowing him he'd bend her over the white plastic table and spank her ass raw if she tried.

And it was the threat of what he would do that kept her from telling him to go to Hell.

Damn him! Why was he doing this to her? She'd never met a man as tenacious as him.

She'd thought the fact that she'd had sex with his friend would send him running to Borno State, the farthest State from Rivers State where she lived or to somewhere else equally far away. She'd expected him to avoid her like she was a leper. Any Nigerian man who saw his potential girlfriend do something like that would react in that manner, right?

Not Tope. He sat across from her, grinning like a man who'd won the Lotto and introducing her to people as his wife.

For fuck sake, she wasn't his wife. Would never be anybody's wife.

What did she have to do to make him see that? What was wrong with him? Why did her audacious behaviour not put him off? Why the fuck wasn't he angry that she'd fucked Bosco?

She'd been expecting anger and disgust from Tope. But none of it came.

Even when he'd spanked her, he hadn't been vexed. Yes, he'd been stern, his voice booming and authoritative. But she hadn't feared for her safety. Just for her sore ass.

Her head swam, her stomach turning to rock.

Tope frightened her. Not because he could harm her physically. But because he seemed to be the first man she couldn't predict. She couldn't figure him out, damn it.

She had to find out what to do to make him leave her alone.

Mama Ejima returned with a bottle of Guinness and two tall clear glasses on a brown plastic tray. She placed them on the table and removed the cap from the bottle with the metal opener tied to a long black sash around her neck.

"Thank you," Tope said as he looked at Anuli, his dark gaze flashing a warning.

"Thank you," Anuli said and shifted in her seat. Her bum wasn't as sore at it was earlier but it still held heat.

The woman beamed a smile at her before asking, "Wetin you go chop? We get Buru Folu, Banga, Egusi, even Edikaikon. Abi na rice and stew you want?"

Another quick glance at Tope showed he was watching her, although she couldn't tell if he'd be angry if she didn't order any food. She was hungry but the thought of sitting here, pretending to be his wife made her skin prickle.

"I no know," she said, choosing to play it safe. "Make you ask Oga Tope first, eh."

"Make you bring Buru Folu, bring pounded yam. I go feed iyawo mi from my own." He flashed another of his wicked smile.

Anuli's skin pricked again at the idea of him feeding her, which would only cement her status as his wife in the eyes of onlookers.

"I no wan chop pounded yam," she said quickly. "Abeg bring me ofada rice with assorted meat stew."

"No wahala," Mama Ejima said before sauntering off.

"So you were hungry after all." Tope smirked as he poured the black liquid into a tilted glass, letting one settle as he filled the other before topping both of them up.

Her heart thudded in her chest. They shared a love of Guinness Stout. It was the only beer she drank. Anyway, there was no point getting carried away. It didn't mean anything. Just coincidence.

He picked up one full glass and placed it in front of her.

"Thanks." She lifted it and inhaled. The smell of roasted malts, coffee and caramel filled her nostrils just as she took a sip of the dark liquid, savouring the creamy taste of dark chocolate with a hint of sweetness.

Her eyes drifted shut and she rolled her tongue over her upper lip. "Mmmmhh."

"You like the drink, then." Tope's deep amused voice made her open her eyes. "I did something right."

He smiled at her, a genuine expression of pleasure. She couldn't help smiling back. He had done something right. She couldn't take it away from him.

"Yes. I like Guinness. It's the only beer I drink."

"Really? I didn't know that." He looked surprised as he took a sip from his drink. "I've learned something new about you. What else do you like?"

She leaned back in her seat. "Why do you want to know?"

He shrugged. "I want to know what you like so I know how to make you happy. Isn't that what a good husband is supposed to do?"

"We're back to that again. You do realise that we're not really married, right? For one, you haven't proposed to me or even paid dowry or anything."

"We could rectify that easily. Tell me where your people are and I'll go and pay your bride price."

Her chest tightened. She wasn't ever going to let the money-grabbing fools who called themselves her relatives to ever get anything called bride price on her account.

"I don't have any family."

He leaned forward and covered her hand with his, his expression sobering. "I'm sorry."

She tugged her hand free. "Why are you sorry? Is it your fault that I have a bunch of assholes as relatives? Anyway, you're supposed to propose to me first."

He stared at her silently for several heartbeats. "I would propose to you, if I knew you would accept me. You don't trust me. I understand that. But I want you to get to know me and trust me. There's something between us. Something intense and powerful. You need to admit it to yourself."

She smiled slowly, seductively, knowing what it was he wanted from her. "The only thing between us is lust. Nothing more. You're just like this because we haven't had sex."

He moved his chair to sit beside her and lowered his voice as he whispered in her ear. "You think this is about sex? I could've fucked you while we were at Bosco's. I could've buried myself deep in your ass while he fucked your pussy. I could've made you take my cock in your mouth. I could've covered your body with cum. And you would've loved every minute of it."

The tip of his finger trailed a path down her thigh under the table.

Shit. Her heart raced, thudding hard against her chest. Heat flushed her skin as her nipples pebbled, chaffing against her bra. Her pussy creamed, her inside contracting at the pictures his words painted. She wanted the reality. Tope, Bosco, together.

"But this isn't about sex, Tiger." He withdrew his hand and she nearly shouted at him to put it back on her body. "Sure, I want you and I'm going to fuck you. But that's not all I want. I want everything you have to offer, heart, body and soul and I'm going to get it."

He picked up his drink.

She sucked in a deep breath to get her heart to slow down and swallowed the lump in her throat. "So you're going to keep telling people I'm your wife and refuse to let me go home? That's kidnapping."

His jaw tightened and it took a few seconds before he responded. "If that's what it takes to make you accept this thing between us, then I'll keep you locked up."

Chapter Seven

"I'll keep you locked up."

Those words rattled in Anuli's head as she ate the food when Mama Ejima brought it. So many thoughts bounced in her head that she barely tasted the food although she usually enjoyed the local rice and spicy tomato stew.

Her gaze ping-ponged around the room and she stayed quiet, not bothering to engage in discussions. She couldn't shake the sinking feeling or the heaviness in her body.

How did today go so wrong? How did she go from being ready to slay her demons to being trapped with Tope?

Any other time, she would have been cool about hanging out with him. She would've even made him pay for the time with her if he wanted her that badly. She hadn't fucked a man for money in weeks aside from Bosco. Even that didn't count as the man hadn't even finished, although she'd climaxed with Tope's interference.

Her total focus was on the one goal—getting rid of Uncle Joe.

She wouldn't enjoy anything else until that man was literally dead to her.

Now Tope was scuppering her plans. The man in question was totally at ease, even having conversations with other patrons.

She thought about getting up and walking out of the restaurant at one point. It wasn't too late to get a bus or motorbike back to her place. But Tope had one arm slung over the back of her chair in a possessive gesture and she doubted she would've gotten far before he apprehended her.

Not wanting to incur any more chastisement, she decided to bide her time. If he thought she would just let him detain her without a fight, then he was in for a surprise.

She had escaped from Uncle Joe. She could certainly escape from Tope. She just had to make him think she'd given up on getting away. When he let his guard down as he was going to do at some point, she would strike.

Although to be fair, aside from the obsession Tope seemed to have with her, there was no similarities between him and Uncle Joe.

She couldn't imagine Tope imprisoning young girls as sex slaves and pimping them out to other men.

No. If she'd even gotten a hint that Tope was as evil as her stepfather, she would put a bullet through him first before finding Uncle Joe and killing him.

This was the reason she couldn't be distracted with Tope, no matter how rough and ready he looked. No matter how much she wanted him to bend her over and fuck her so hard her legs wouldn't hold her up. No matter how much she sat here dripping with arousal and aching for him.

No, she couldn't stay. She had to find Uncle Joe and end his miserable life. She knew for certain that a man like him would have found another girl or girls to turn into sex slaves. She couldn't let him get away with what he had done, which was likely to happen even with an ongoing investigation. Who ever heard of paedophiles being prosecuted and imprisoned in Nigeria? It didn't happen. She wasn't holding out any hope on that happening, no matter how much Tessa and Peter reassured her it would happen.

They had good intentions but Anuli had never believed in white knights. She had rescued herself from Uncle Joe as a child and taken Tessa with her. She certainly wasn't waiting for anybody to give her justice for the childhood she'd lost because of that man.

She would deliver justice for herself.

First, she needed to escape from Tope. Shame. She was sure a few days with him, screwing each other until they were boneless, would work wonders for both her and him.

Any woman who liked men who were rough and tough would certainly swoon at the thought of being with a man like Tope. To be honest, sitting here watching him lick soup off his fingers, her panties got wet imagining it was her body he was licking.

He met her gaze and her heart flipped over.

There was soup smudged on the corner of his mouth. Before she could stop herself, she reached out and swiped it off with her left index finger. She'd been used to swiping stuff off Tessa's skin so it came naturally to her to do it without thinking.

Tope grabbed her wrist with his left hand and brought her finger to his mouth. He swiped his rough, warm tongue over her skin.

Tingles shot down her arm straight to her clit. Her pulse shot off into space and she had to suppress a moan.

"*Tope.*" His name slipped from her lips in a plea. She wanted him to lick her again.

"I love it when you say my name," he said in a low voice as he stroked her wrist. He must feel the fast thumping of her pulse where he held her. He leaned close to her ear. "I can't wait to fuck you."

He lowered her hand to cover his bulge under the table. He felt hot, hard. Huge.

"Why don't we get out of here?" she said in a breathy voice while she squeezed his jeans-covered erection.

He sucked in a sharp breath before tilting his head sideways to look at her face. "You weren't in a hurry to get to mine earlier. What changed?"

"This." She squeezed his dick again and leaned into him. "Take me home and fuck me."

His eyes darkened as he leaned back and raised his free hand. "Mama Ejima, bring my bill."

He dipped the same hand in the blue plastic bowl of clean water and washed it before drying it with the paper towel. Then he reached in his pocket and pulled out his brown leather wallet. All this while, his other hand was holding hers over his bulge as if he didn't want her to stop touching him.

Mama Ejima came over and told him the price. He took notes out and handed them to the woman. "Keep the change."

"Thank you," she replied before saying to Anuli. "I hope say you enjoy the food."

"I enjoy am. Thank you," Anuli replied.

"Good night." Tope didn't release her hand and pulled her up as he stood.

Anuli followed him back out to the car where he repeated the same thing he'd done earlier, helping her climb into the SUV before walking around to the driver's side. If she didn't know better, she'd think he was a gentleman.

"Why are you always opening the door for me?" she asked when he joined her in the car.

He leaned back to pull on his seat belt. "One of the first things I learned from watching my parents was seeing my father open the door for my mother every time they went out together. He wasn't a rich man or anything. He was a taxi driver and drove a Peugeot 504 that had seen better days. But every time they went out together, which was mostly on Sundays to church, he would wait for her to come out, open the door to the front passenger seat and close it when she was seated."

"Really?" She raised her brow. "I never thought Nigerian men did that. My stepfather was never like that."

"I suppose it was my father's thing. I asked him once why he did it and he said, 'Son, when you find the woman who will be your wife, treat her like a queen, so that she can treat you like a king.' It was one of the best advice he ever gave me."

Her heart clutched tight. She was all for men treating women like queens. If only more men would be like that. "Your father is a very wise man."

"Was," he said in a sombre tone. "My father was a wise man. He died a few years ago. He was heartbroken when my mother died. She was everything to him. He died a year after she died, almost to the day."

"Wow. I'm so sorry." She reached out and covered his hand on the gear stick. She'd never known relationships like that. Her father had died when she was too young to remember him.

"Thank you," he said as he lifted her hand to his lips. "I miss him and I wish he was around to meet you. He was a no-nonsense disciplinarian."

"Now I know where you learned to be strict." She gave a wry smile.

He chuckled. "Yeah. He made sure we didn't go off the rails. But he also had a soft side. My mum brought that out in him. I think you do the same thing for me. You smooth out my rough edges, just like sandpaper on rough wood."

"You're saying I'm sandpaper?" she pouted.

He chuckled as he kissed her knuckles, sending tingles down her spine. "I'm saying that if anything happened to you, I'll be heartbroken. This is the reason you have to tell me why you bought a gun. Did someone threaten you? Are you in danger?"

A chill ran down her spine. She stiffened, pulled her hand out of his grasp and turned away, staring in the direction of the buka. She didn't want to discuss her plans. He would only try to convince her not to do it or even give himself more reason to keep her with him.

"Anuli, you have to talk to me."

"Will you give me back the gun if I tell you?"

"Maybe. Depends on why you want it."

"Not good enough."

"You're going to have to tell me sometime." He puffed out a deep breath and started the car engine.

She didn't reply, knowing it was probably true. But if she didn't tell him, then she still had some leverage.

It turned out his house wasn't far from the restaurant. They drove about a hundred yards from the restaurant and turned right into a bumpy unpaved side road for another few hundred yards before he stopped in front of grey metal gates and high walls with razor wires at the top.

Tope left the car running with the headlamps on as he got out and unlocked the heavy padlock. The metal grated as he pulled the barriers aside before getting back into the car to drive through onto the concrete driveway. He pulled up under a car port, switched off the engine. They were surrounded by darkness, thanks to the power cut.

"I'm just going to lock the gates." He opened the glove compartment and pulled out a brown parcel and a hand torch. He handed her the flashlight. "Hold on to this."

She turned it on as he got out and walked back to lock the gates. She climbed out too and followed him so she could hold the light for him to see what he was doing. When he finished, he straightened and took the torch from her, placing his arm around her shoulders.

Then he pointed the light in the direction of the white single-level house set on a medium-sized plot. "Welcome to my home."

"You live here on your own." It was a big house for a single man. She'd expected him to be in similar accommodation to Bosco. Instead, she stared at a bungalow suited more to a family home. The area around the house was paved with concrete and there were narrow spaces to the sides leading to the back of the property.

"Yes. It's mine. I bought the land and constructed the house with the help of builders. It took two years to complete. It was only finished a few months ago. Come on. I'll take you inside and turn on the generator."

She grimaced. "Can we skip the generator? I'm not a fan of the noise."

"Okay," he said. "The generator has its own housing so it's not so loud. But we can do without it tonight."

His cool palm covered her nape and he massaged her hot skin. Her breath hitched, her breathing coming quickly afterward.

His right hand covered her hip, pulling her to him as he kissed her.

There was nothing sweet about this kiss as his tongue parted her lips aggressively and swamped her mouth. He held her head and invaded her mouth, like a conqueror.

This man seemed to know what she needed. His fierce need sparked a flame inside her.

Her eyelids drifted shut. Answering arousal flared in her veins. She couldn't hold back. She gripped his shoulders and pulled herself up, wrapping her legs around his hips, squashing her boobs on his chest.

"Fuck." He broke the kiss, his harsh breathing washing over her cheeks. He palmed her ass, holding her up as he took steps towards the house. "I can't wait."

"You don't have to wait." She could barely get air into her lungs. She brought her right hand down between their bodies and tugged at the belt holding his jeans up. "It's your house and no one else is around."

"You read my mind." His white teeth flashed in the low light as he almost staggered onto the veranda and dropped the items in his hands on the floor. She heard the clatter of keys and the thump of the rubber flashlight. The place pitched into darkness. The only light came from the starry sky.

She dropped her bag and fumbled with his belt as her back hit a wall. Then his fingers were on her jeans, tugging at the buttons. He returned to kissing her, his tongue sweeping savagely as they competed to see who would undress the other first.

She managed to get his zipper down and reach between the parted denim to find stretchy cotton boxer-briefs covering him.

He yanked at her jeans, popping the last button, distracting her. She kicked off her shoes as he tugged the jeans off. Something pinged against the concrete as she lifted her hips to help him remove the offending material.

As soon as his palm covered her mound through her lace undies, she sighed in relief, eager for the skin to skin contact that was to come.

"You're so hot. So wet. I can feel it on your panties." His gruff voice whispered against her skin. He stroked a finger up and down against the fabric.

She keened, her hips canting.

"You like me touching you." His callused left hand gripped her nape, the right one stroking her pussy. "Say it."

"Yes, I do. I like your hands on my body." She bit her lip to stop from begging him to touch her directly and not just through the fabric.

He did it anyway, his fingers sliding under the lace and driving into her slick opening.

"Yes! More. More," she demanded as she writhed.

He obliged her, thrusting three large, rough fingers in and out of her while his thumb grazed her clit, her wetness coating his skin. She rode his hand, her hips tilting with his rhythm even as his other hand held her to the wall, restraining her with his strength.

Her skin tingled and warmth spread out from her core as her orgasm detonated, fever sweeping through her.

She was still in a daze when he withdrew his hand. Panting to catch her breath, she collapsed onto his shoulder, sweat making her blouse stick to her flesh.

He reached in his back pocket for something and then the crackling sound of a condom wrapper mixed with the evening cricket song. He shoved his jeans down and she heard the rubber rolling onto his erection.

When she'd caught her breath, she raised her head and grinned at him, only for her smile to die as he lined up the broad head of his dick with her slit and rammed in.

She slammed against the wall and her body bowed in pleasure.

"Ohhhh," she moaned at being filled so snugly with his heavy shaft.

He pounded into her savagely, her back hitting against the wall again and again. She was going to be sore. But she didn't care. Not with the pleasure erupting all over body. She needed a little bit of pain with her pleasure. She needed the reminder that she was alive and kicking. That she was human. Female. Desirable.

She wanted to forget the past. She wanted to be fucked until everything in her life was blurred and all she felt was the sensation of here and now.

Tope gave it to her, somehow knowing what she wanted without her vocalising it. Every nerve ending inside her sparked to life. He lifted her bum, angling the thrusts so that he hit her sweet spot over and over. His hand on her neck tightened, just as the one on her hip did too.

"Tope," she sang his name in ecstasy. Her skin tingled, the sensation spreading. She gulped in air, lungs expanding and collapsing as adrenaline flowed and ebbed.

She dug her nails into his shoulders. He didn't seem to mind that she was hurting him. She floated in space, into a happy place as orgasm came seconds after orgasm.

"Fuck. I'm coming." He grunted and slammed in one last time before his body jerked in spasms.

They clung to each other, his body pressed to hers against the wall. After a few seconds to recover, he staggered backwards and sat on the low veranda wall, keeping her on top of him. He pressed his sweat-slicked forehead against hers.

"This is a good way to come home." There was amusement in his voice.

She giggled. "Yeah. It is. But you're going to have to carry me over the threshold as I can't walk."

She realised what she'd said after it was out. New brides were carried over the threshold. Her statement would make him think she'd agreed to whatever this relationship was supposed to be.

He lifted his head and tugged her chin up. His face was in shadows but she saw the query in his eyes.

"I'd be happy to carry you over the threshold, Tiger. Any day." He shifted her to sit on the cool wall. "Stay here for minute. Let me open the door. Then I'll carry you in."

He groped around the floor until he found the items he'd abandoned. With the flashlight back on and keys in hand, he opened the door and went inside.

She found her jeans and pulled them back on but didn't bother with her shoes. She held them in her hands along with her bag. She stood at the door when he appeared with the torch.

"I told you to wait," he said, bending forward to pick her up.

She stepped away although her legs wobbled. "There's no need. I can walk."

His frown showed he wasn't happy but he didn't say anything. Light illuminated a white-walled hallway with doors leading off it. She stepped into the cool interior. He shut the door, twisting the lock into place.

"This way." He led her through a door on the right. He fiddled with something on a table and the room filled with light from a battery-powered lamp.

It was a sitting room with mink-coloured upholstered chairs and dark wood centre table and sides tables. A widescreen TV sat on an entertainment unit that matched the tables. Large grey speakers sat on either side of the unit.

"I can show you the rest of the place," he said from behind her.

She turned around, took a step so their bodies collided. "You can start by showing me your bedroom."

Chapter Eight

Sunlight beamed through the slits of closed shutters as Anuli woke. It took a few seconds for her eyes to adjust. She was in a large room with dark wood furniture and her body caged by the solid mass of muscles and limbs.

Her body ached, a good ache, her pussy sore from taking a lot of pounding. She stretched, yawned.

Had she overslept with a client? It never happened. She was usually up and out of their hotel rooms by the first light of dawn. Even if she didn't wake, her alarm woke her.

The sun was already up. This room didn't exactly look like a hotel room. And she hadn't worked for weeks as she focused on her new goal.

So who was this? She turned her head to look at the man. She recognised his face, skin of dark-roasted coffee. Dark lashes like crescent feathers on his angular cheeks, not to mention the full, firm lips framed by neatly trimmed hair and that knew how to work her body as much as the rest of him. Tope.

They'd had sex. First on the veranda, then in the bedroom. The man was strong and fierce. Insatiable. She'd lost count at how many times she'd come after the fifth one. He'd woken her several times in the night, hard and ready for her. He'd held her down, pounding into her until she practically melted into the mattress.

A plastic bottle of water sat on the night stand. She'd asked for some water sometime in the night and he'd gone to get it for her. After each round, he'd cradled her, much like he was doing now.

She didn't cuddle and she'd tried to wriggle out but had given up in the end. He didn't let her go. She had to admit that his powerful arms and body felt good against her.

Sighing, she closed her eyes. Maybe now that he'd sated himself with sex, he'd let her go home. He would have to be at work on Monday so he had to let her go then, surely. She dozed off with that thought in her mind.

Next time she woke, she was alone in bed, crisp blue cotton sheet covering her naked body. She swung her legs over the side of the wooden bed frame and her feet settled on cool floor tiles. She shivered as the sheet slipped off her body and crisp air touched her skin. It must have rained sometime early this morning.

Her clothes that had been strewn all over the floor when they'd come for round two in the bedroom were now in a pile over an armchair in the corner.

"Good morning, Tiger. You're awake."

She lifted her head as Tope walked into the room, beaming a smile and dressed in green cargo shorts and white T-shirt.

Jeez. He was a dark chocolate hulk of a man. She bit her lower lip as her core throbbed. She wanted to take another bite into him.

"Erm. Morning. I was just thinking of getting dressed and going home," she replied, reaching for her clothes.

She had to get out of here before she turned into one of those women who drooled over men. Last night had been a brief moment of madness.

He strode past her as if he didn't hear her, opened the top drawer in a wide wooden chest and withdrew a folded white T-shirt. He flipped it to unfold it and turned around, a grin still on his face.

"Let's put this on you. Then you can brush your teeth and come and have breakfast." He pulled her up from the bed.

Well, he wasn't saying she couldn't go home. So she could live with it. She tugged her arm free and reached for the shirt. "I can do it."

"No, let me." He smiled as he lifted the outfit over her head. "Remember, you're my queen."

He winked at her, the corner of his right eye crinkled and his lips tugged up in a lopsided smile. Warmth bloomed across her chest.

On the days she'd seen him at work in Park Hotel, his dark eyes had sent a tremor down her spine with its mix of darkness and intensity.

Now they held warmth, tenderness and humour, something she'd never really associated with him before.

Standing so close to him, she could smell his scent, his spice. Even a hint of her scent on him. His hands on her skin as he lowered the shirt over her head only ramped up her awareness of him.

"You do know that if I were a queen, I wouldn't be one of those ajebutter prim and proper ones who sit around all day. I would be bored out of my brain," she said as she slipped her arms through the sleeves. The fabric fell, cotton grazing her already pebbled nipples.

He stepped close, breaching the gap between them. His gaze snagged hers, the raw emotion blazed.

"No. My tiger wouldn't be a simpering queen being waited on hand and foot. You would be a warrior queen, out on the battle field with your king and his knights, slaying dragons and demons."

Shit. Her breath locked tight in her throat. How did this man know her so well? It was both captivating and terrifying to have someone unravel her so easily. The only person who'd ever understood her was Tessa. Even Tessa didn't know everything about her.

Tope seemed to learn her with such ease.

Fuck. She needed to get out of here. She didn't want anyone in her head. Let alone this man.

She took a step back. He matched her step as if they were doing a dance.

His left hand went to her nape, his right hand on her hip, bringing their bodies in line again. Bullet point nipples poked his chest just as his bulge prodded her belly through the fabrics.

"Do you know why I nicknamed you Tiger?" His voice had a deep quality that reverberated inside her.

"Because I was wearing a tiger-striped print dress the other day?" she answered in a flippant tone.

His eyes twinkled before becoming intense. "No. That's not it. Tigers are powerful and strong. So are you. You're not afraid of anything. And I like that. You shouldn't fear anyone. Not even me."

"Really?" She barked out a short laugh as she remembered the spanking he'd given her last night. "My sore bum begs to disagree after yesterday."

"No. Me spanking you isn't about fear. It's about respect. You shouldn't fear me. But you should respect me. In fact, as my queen, I demand your respect just as I give you respect."

"You demand it?" She stiffened, hands balled, and tilted her chin up to glare at him.

"Yes, I do. Have I shown you any disrespect in the time you've known me?"

"You took my gun away and refuse to give it back to me. That's disrespectful."

His grip on her nape tightened. "Do you have a gun license?"

Her face puckered in a frown, his question catching her off balance. She hadn't been expecting a question like that. Hadn't even thought about applying for a gun license. "N—no."

"If you get stopped and searched by the police and they find the gun, what will happen?"

Her frown deepened and her cheeks smarted. She lowered her gaze, her body going limp.

He used his thumb to push her chin up so she had to look up at his face. He had the stern expression from yesterday. The one that made him appear authoritative and hypnotizing all at the same time. Her bum tingled as she remembered his huge, sharp palm making contact.

"Answer me."

"I guess I'll be arrested," she said in a stiff voice.

"Yes, you'll be arrested and detained as an armed robber or kidnapper or some other criminal charge as well as possession of a deadly weapon."

"But it wouldn't have happened. The police won't arrest me. I'll be careful."

"Really? The same way you were careful when you were asking around for where to buy a gun? Do you know what kind of man Mike Ocha is? He would sell his mother for profit. He would have double crossed you if I hadn't intervened. He would've taken your money and still gotten you arrested so he could get the gun back."

She stiffened. She'd known Mike Ocha was a dangerous man and not to be trusted. In fact, she'd been sort of happy when he'd referred her to Bosco. Although she didn't know Bosco, she'd thought anyone would've been better than the slime ball of a man.

"I would have gotten back at him for double crossing me after I got out of the police cell."

"But you wouldn't have known Mike was the one who betrayed you. Anyway, my point is that I took the gun away from you because it is safer in my hands than in yours."

She opened her mouth to speak but he continued.

"Before you say anything. Yes, I'm licensed to carry a weapon. Not to mention that I'm actually trained to use the weapons and to protect lives. So no, I'm not disrespecting you by keeping the gun. I'm protecting you even if you refuse to see it."

"Fine. Keep the gun." She would just have to find another way of getting a hold of it, even if it meant tearing his house down.

He leaned down and brushed his lips on her forehead, the curly hairs of his beard tickled her nose. He stepped back and his right hand tapped her bum.

"Ouch," she yelped. It was more a shock than painful.

He grinned and flicked his hand, shooing her. "Go on. Get into the bathroom and come out for breakfast. Five minutes."

She didn't even bother arguing about the fact that he was commanding her to brush her teeth and even timing her on top of it.

She sashayed to the door and then turned her head to glance at him. "You know a queen cannot be rushed. I could be all day in the bathroom."

He shook his head. "Not when her king is hungry. If you're not out in time, I'll be breaking the bathroom door down and warming your ass up nicely."

"You're a tyrant, you know."

"Me, a tyrant. Oya, wait." He strode across the room.

She yelped again and hurried down the hallway into the bathroom he'd shown her last night and shut the door. She leaned on the slab, catching her breath as she tried not to laugh.

"Why are you running?" he asked from the other side of the closed door, his voice filled with humour.

"Because my bum needs to cool down, not warm up, abeg," she replied, unable to hold back laughter.

He laughed too before saying, "There's a new toothbrush on the sink for you. Remember, five minutes or I'm coming back and the door won't protect you."

She heard the steady slap of his bare feet on the hard floor as he retreated.

The grin was still on her face as she turned around, her body warm and tingly.

In the daylight, the white tiles on the wall and floor dazzled. A white tub sat to her left. It had a small electric water heater unit on the wall above it which worked for the shower and the bath taps. A water closet of the same colour sat at the end wall below the small window with mottled glass which let the light in but provided an opaque view. She could see the silhouette of trees against the blue sky.

She stepped up to the white sink which sat on the opposite wall to the bath and saw her reflection in the mirrored cabinet above it. Her face was lit up, her eyes twinkling, her lips pulled up in a smile. Her hair was in disarray although she's managed to pull it back into a bun before she slept. Loose strands stuck out in all directions around her. She looked like a woman who'd gotten exactly what she'd wanted. A woman who'd been thoroughly fucked until she buzzed and glowed.

Sex with Tope had been awesome. In her scorecard, he would be an A-plus star. The man didn't do things by halves.

She sighed. A few more hours, perhaps a day of so with him wouldn't hurt. She could put her plans on hold for now. She would spend the time with Tope, fuck like wild animals until they got tired of each other, which was bound to happen. Then he'd let her go home and she would get on with her plans.

The toothbrush was exactly where he said it would be. She popped it out of the plastic wrapper and pressed some toothpaste from the red and white tube on the sink. She brushed her teeth as she thought of all the hot, sweaty, filthy sex she could have with Tope.

A huge grin spread her lips as she turned on the chrome tap. Cool water poured out and she splashed water on her face before rinsing out the toothbrush and placing it back on the ceramic surface.

She took steps to the door, turned the handle and pulled the slab back. Her heart thudded in her chest.

Tope stood in the hallway, facing her, his expression unreadable. "Your time is up."

Chapter Nine

"Hey. I'm not late, am I? It can't be more than five minutes already," Anuli protested as she stood her ground. It couldn't have been that long since she went into the bathroom.

Tope lifted his wrist and pressed a button on the rose-plated wrist watch with a black dial and black rubber strap. The chunky design was eye-catching and stylish.

"Four minutes and fifty-one seconds," he said with a grin. "You cut it close. Come on."

He put an arm around her shoulders and guided her down the corridor.

She looked up sideways at him. "You were actually timing me. Damn."

He flashed another grin full of white teeth. "I'm a man of my word. The key to earning your trust is to remain consistent and to keep to my word. How are you ever going to trust me if I say one thing and do another?"

"But it's only a little thing. I was only using the bathroom. What difference would it make if I stayed ten minutes in there and you let me off?" she asked as he ushered her into the dining room end of the living space.

He pulled out a chair and waited for her to settle before taking the seat next to her on the left, at the head of the six-seat table. The table and chairs were made from the same dark wood, although the chairs were cushioned and covered in the same mink fabric as the sofas.

"The same rules apply across the board," he said, elbows braced on the table surface. "That's what integrity is about. If you can't trust me with the little things, you can never trust me with the big thing. It's the difference between life and death in my line of work."

Her stomach twisted. "But that's harsh. You're always going to punish me every time I step out of line."

He met her gaze, his open. He wasn't hiding himself from her. "I will never be cruel to you. My punishments will always match the offense. So for example, if you'd been one minute over the five minutes, you would've receive one smack to the bum. Two minutes, two smacks, etc."

"Fair enough. But still, can't you just let me off anyway? You say I bring out the soft side. You should just forgive me," she said, pushing her luck.

"I do forgive you after the punishment has been administered." He chuckled. "Seriously though, ask yourself and be honest. Do you want a soft man? Do you want a pushover? A man you can easily control. He's not going to keep your interest more than a few days."

"That's if he lasts that long," she replied without thinking, unable to hide her disgust at having to live with such a man. She shuddered and met his gaze. She realised her words had just proved his point so she added. "Anyway, I've always thought men were only good for one thing. Sex. I don't hang around for anything else."

He looked at his watch again. "It's been at least five hours since our last round of sex and you're still here. So I must be doing something right."

"Yeah, that's because you promised me breakfast." She winked at him.

He chuckled and shook his head. "Yes, I did promise. So get eating, then."

She lifted the lid from the brown ceramic bowl in the middle of the table. Steam rose from the egg stew as he opened the other bowl to reveal steaming yam slices.

"I wasn't sure if you preferred coffee or tea so I brought out both of them." Tope pointed to the jars of coffee granules and tea bags. "There's hot water in the flask."

"Coffee is fine." She popped the lid of the metal tin with her teaspoon and scooped some granules into the brown mug, before pouring hot water from the stainless steel flask.

Breakfast went by easily, the conversation between them flowing effortlessly as if they were used to sitting down and eating meals together. As if they were a couple.

She tried not to dwell on that revealing notion, on the idea that she could really become a couple with Tope. That they could sit down together every Sunday morning and eat breakfast after a night of fulfilling sex. That she could enjoy a man's company enough to stay beyond the sex.

After breakfast, she finally made it into the kitchen as she helped to clear up. Interesting that he stood with her as she washed up the dishes and he put them away. With his commanding attitude, she'd expected that he would leave the washing up to her. But just like he hadn't waited for her to cook the breakfast, he didn't seem bothered about helping out with cleaning up either.

A bell buzzed as she wiped down the counter with the napkin. She wondered how someone had gotten past the locked gates. "Is that the door bell?"

"No." He put the last plate on the shelf. "It's from the gate. There's a bell installed beside it for visitors."

It made sense since he lived alone and didn't have a gateman.

"I'll go and see who it is." He pulled opened a drawer and took out a bunch of keys before heading to the front door.

Curious to see what kind of people visited him, she followed but waited on the veranda as he walked up the short drive to the gate.

He had a short discussion with whoever was on the other side, although she couldn't see the person from this far. Then the clanking of padlock, keys and chains filled the air before he pulled the gates ajar.

A young boy probably twelve or thirteen years old walked through and greeted him. He was in a green shirt and matching shorts.

Tope locked up the gates and the two of them walked towards the veranda.

"Anuli, this is Nonso, one half of the twins."

"Good morning, Aunty," Nonso greeted, bowing slightly.

"Morning, Nonso," she replied pleasantly but turned to Tope. "Half of whose twins?"

"Mama Ejima's twins." He chuckled.

"Oh. Of course." She smiled. Which other twins would it be since Mama Ejima translated to 'mother of twins'? "How your mum?"

"She dey fine, Aunty. She say make I come sweep Oga Tope house."

Tope coughed. "Nonso, you know the rules in this house."

The boy's eyes went wide and he stiffened as if he'd been caught doing something wrong. "Yes, sir. I'm sorry, sir."

"I'll let you off this time. Go inside and do your chores," Tope said, sounding like the boy's father.

Nonso nodded and hurried indoors.

"What was that about?" Anuli asked, baffled.

"Nonso isn't allowed to speak Pidgin English while he's in my house," Tope said as he leaned against the wall next to the door. Last night, he'd had her up against the very same wall.

She sucked in a deep breath and tried to concentrate on what he was saying.

"It's not that I have anything against him speaking pidgin but outside of these walls, he has little opportunity to speak the Queen's English since 'Broken' is the common language in the neighbourhood."

"But why is it your business if he speaks proper English or not?" She really couldn't stand

100

busybodies and hoped that wasn't what Tope was to these people.

"Nonso's father isn't around and his mother is raising the kids alone. Do you know how difficult that is? She's taken me like a younger brother. She sends the boy over every weekend to clean the house or run errands for me. In turn, I treat her and the kids like family. I'm the big uncle. I give him and his sister pocket money. I take interest in their studies. He's a smart kid but there was a time when he played truant and skipped school for a while, hanging out with street kids. I soon taught him the error of his ways. I make him show me his school reports and he gets rewarded for doing well. Same as his sister."

Anuli sat on the low wall of the veranda, speechless as she listened to Tope. Wow. He was something else. An adult who cared about a child who wasn't his.

As a child, all the adults around her had failed her. None of them had taken any interest in her plight or what happened to her after her mother died. If any of them knew what was happening to her, none of them intervened.

Tope was an adult who cared about a boy who wasn't his or even a relative. He was determined not to fail this child. He was determined to see this child walk the right path. To keep the child out of danger. She could see it in his eyes as he spoke.

What if someone like Tope had cared about her as a child? Her life wouldn't have turned out the way it did.

Something unravelled inside her. A flutter in her belly. Her breath felt bottled up in her chest as she gently bit her lip. Before she knew what she was doing, she stood and walked across the space. She pressed her body up against Tope's and stood on tiptoes.

He seemed surprised at her action but didn't stop her as she pressed her mouth to his.

She stepped back after a brief kiss, breathing deeply.

"Thank you," she said in a breathy voice.

"Why are you thanking me?" He still appeared baffled.

"For what you are doing for this kid. If someone had taken an interest in me as a child, maybe..." she trailed off and stepped back.

He reached for her and tugged her into his arms, giving her a tight hug. He didn't say anything but nothing needed to be said. It was just great being held and feeling as if someone cared even if it was about fifteen years too late.

Chapter Ten

Anuli's decision to stay for one day at Tope's stretched to days. A week later and she was still at his. His revelations about Nonso and Mama Ejima had floored her more than anything else he'd done and said. The thought of refusing Tope anything after that felt selfish.

It wasn't as if she never left his house during the following days.

On the Sunday, after Nonso had finished cleaning and left, she'd showered and dressed in the clothes she'd worn the previous day. Tope had offered to drive her to her place to pick up some clothes.

She'd taken up his offer. When they'd arrived at hers, she'd grabbed the bag she'd partially packed in preparation for her trip. She'd stuffed the extra items she'd needed for a few days into it.

Of course, observant Tope had asked why she'd had a bag already packed. She'd told him she'd been planning to take a trip but hadn't expanded on her destination. He didn't push it.

Later that evening when they returned to his, he'd informed her she would be accompanying him to work. Apparently, the Housekeeping team was short-staffed and needed extra pairs of hands as there was a conference booked in the hotel for the week and all the rooms were booked. She'd balked at the idea of returning to Park Hotel.

But then he'd said, "Remember you're the queen who doesn't want to be waited on hand and foot. You don't want to sit in my house all week getting bored, do you?"

To that, she didn't have a comeback.

So Monday morning, she'd dressed and gotten in the car with him to Park Hotel. He'd escorted her to the manager's office and waited for her to apologise to the man for all her unauthorised absences.

She'd felt like a pupil marched to the headmaster's office for misbehaviour. But apologising to Christopher was easier than bending over Tope's lap and having her butt spanked, which was what he promised if she didn't show remorse. Of course, Tope also reminded her that now his reputation was on the line if she misbehaved at work.

So she'd worked every day that he'd worked. She had actually enjoyed being busy. She was never meant to sit around doing nothing. She loved physical activity. Cleaning hotel rooms kept her busy.

On Friday, she walked outside the back of the premises where some of the staff hung out during their breaks. Some of the women stopped talking when she walked by. She knew they must have been talking about her.

She stiffened her posture and walked to a corner where another girl she was friendly with sat on a bench smoking. Anuli hadn't smoked since she'd been with Tope. She was a social smoker. But the gossiping girls wound her up.

"Rose, abeg borrow me one ciga. I go give you back another time," she said.

"No wahala," Rose replied and pulled the pack out of her pocket.

Anuli lifted one out and popped it in her mouth, bending forward when Rose flicked the blue plastic lighter on. She crossed her legs, bent her elbow on her lap and took a long drag, sucking in the nicotine, letting it settle her nerves. Tilting her head to the side, she blew smoke into the air. It swirled around them before dissipating.

"Wetin them dey talk over there?" Anuli nodded in the direction of the group of girls who kept staring at her as they continued talking.

"You no know? Na you be the topic. You and Oga Tope," Rose replied before taking a puff from her cigarette.

"I figure that one already. I want to know what they are saying."

"No be my mouth you go take hear that one."

"Is it that bad?"

Rose shrugged.

"Okay. I'll go and find out for myself." Anuli dropped her cigarette and stubbed it with her shoe before picking it and throwing it in the trash can as she stood up again.

She strode over to the group of girls. "So I overheard you talking about me. Well, you can say whatever to my face."

Three of the girls turned and looked at her before walking away like they didn't want any trouble. Only one girl stood her ground, hands braced on her hips, glaring at Anuli.

She was a skinny, fair-skinned girl but Anuli suspected her fairness was due to bleaching products rather than Mother Nature, if the dark patches on her knuckles and elbow were any indications. This week had been the first time Anuli had seen the girl and they hadn't spoken to each other until now, but she knew her name as Joy.

"And so? What if we're talking?" Joy snapped.

"Huh?" Anuli reared back and glanced around. "Do you have a problem with me?"

"Yes, I have a problem with you. You walk around as if you own the place. As if your Papa owns Park Hotel." The girl swung her long extensions to the side. "I don't even know what Tope sees in you. You prostitute."

Anuli sucked in a sharp breath. Did the girl know what she'd done for a living or was she just calling her names? In Nigeria, the word 'prostitute' was bandied about as an insulting word for any self-respecting woman so it didn't hurt.

Anyway, she'd never thought about how her past job would impact her job here. She'd done what she needed to do to survive. If Joy wanted to slut-shame her, the girl was in for a surprise. Anuli didn't do shame.

She took a step closer to the girl. "Oh, I see you're jealous because I'm with Tope. He fucked you and dumped you. Now, you want a piece of me. Well, newsflash. He found himself a real woman this time. One who knows how to please him in every way. Get it?"

She snapped her fingers.

The girl's mouth dropped open and she looked as if blood had drained from her face.

"Next time you want to pick a fight, think twice about who to pick on. Yeye dey smell." Anuli hissed before walking away.

The fury stayed with her through the rest of her shift. She'd been stupid for even succumbing to this thing with Tope but it would end tonight.

When she met up with Tope for the drive back to his place, she stayed quiet. She sat stiffly, muscles quivering. Once she got indoors, she went straight to the bedroom and started packing her things into her small suitcase.

"What are you doing?" Tope's voice came from the bedroom door.

"What does it look like I'm doing?" She glanced up and carried on packing, pulling her clothes from the wardrobe. She was being disrespectful but she didn't care.

He walked in to stand beside her. "Why are you packing your bag?"

"Stupid question, don't you think? D'uh?"

"Hey." He gripped her arm and whirled her around to face. "There's no need to insult me."

"What else would I do when your girlfriend picks a fight with me at work?"

107

His brows puckered. "My girlfriend?"

"Yes," she snapped and tugged her arm free. He let her go. "You should've had the decency to tell me you had fucked half the women at Park Hotel and that I was being invited to join your harem of women."

She stomped out of the bedroom to the kitchen.

He followed her and leaned against the counter with his arms crossed over his chest. "What the hell are you talking about?"

She opened the fridge and took out a bottle of water, before pulling a glass down from the cupboard and slamming it on the counter. She poured water into it, lifted it and took a gulp, allowing the cold drink to quench her thirst and sooth her dry throat.

"I'm talking about Joy," she said when the water was all gone.

"Joy?" His frown deepened.

"Yes. She was gossiping about me with some other of the staff. I confronted her and she insinuated that I wasn't good enough for you on top of calling me a prostitute."

His hands dropped and he balled them into fists as he averted his gaze.

She read his movements as a sign of guilt and turned away, walking to the sink to wash out the glass.

"I'm sorry about Joy. I'll talk to her."

She whirled around. "No. I handled her. She'll think twice before crossing my path again. I don't fucking need you to come to my rescue. I can take care of myself."

He lifted his hands in a conciliatory gesture. "I'm sorry. Joy was a mistake. A—"

She lifted her hand in a stop sign. "I don't want to hear it. It doesn't mean anything to me. You don't mean anything to me. I'm going home."

"Anuli." He took a step toward her.

Adrenaline rushed through her along with her rage. She wasn't thinking straight, only filled with an urge to get away from him at all cost.

She swivelled out of his path and grabbed the kitchen knife from the stock. It was a big chopping knife with a wooden handle, wide and flat in the middle and pointed at the tip. "I'm going home and you're not going to stop me. Or I will use this knife."

Tope's eyes narrowed and he shook his head in slow motion.

"Anuli, put the knife down," he instructed, taking a step in her direction.

Holding the knife up, she widened her stance, shifting her leg away from him, ready to run for the door if necessary.

In one swift movement like an attacking cobra, he gripped her wrist. Sharp pain shot down her arm, disorientating her. She let go of the knife and he swiped it with the other. She heard it clatter into the sink.

The sound drove her into action and she lashed out with her left hand, hitting solid flesh. She couldn't lash out a second time as her left hand was pulled back.

He gripped her against the counter, her back to his chest, her arms twisted while his arm braced around her neck in an almost choking hold.

Her heart raced at how easily he'd overpowered her. She tried to gulp air in and her chest hurt from trying to get air into her lungs.

"Are you going to calm down?" he asked in a low voice, his warm breath feathering her skin.

"Go to hell!" she spat out. She was completely immobile from his rigid arm muscles.

"Behave yourself or I'm going to spank you," he growled in her ear.

Something dark and wicked uncurled inside her. He hadn't spanked her since the first day at Bosco's house. She'd missed that show of his authority. His discipline. It had connected her to him. Grounded her. Made her feel as if she belonged. As if he cared about her enough to discipline her. She wanted that feeling again. Wanted to push him until he claimed her rough and hard.

"I'm not afraid of you. You spank like a girl," she taunted.

He moved so quickly, flipping her around, her head spun. She was bent and face down on the central island unit, cool wood on her cheek, hands still held at her back so she couldn't move them.

Something sharp and cold pressed against the base of her spine. Then she heard ripping sound. He was cutting her skirt off.

She tried to wriggle. "What the hell—"

"Don't move."

The crisp warning made her freeze.

He carried on working until her skirt and knickers floated to the floor in tatters. She was bare from the waist down, apart from her shoes. Her bum jutting out in the air. She heard the knife clatter in the stainless sink again.

He released her hands. "Hold onto the edge of the counter."

Without thinking, she did as he ordered. He gripped her thighs, yanked them apart.

Her grip on the edge of the counter tightened, her breath came out in shallow puffs. Her heart was thumping so hard, her chest felt like it would explode. Still, spread out like this and exposed to him, arousal corded inside her, making her bare clit throb. Anticipation made her body tremble.

She didn't know what he was going to do. She cocked her exposed ear. The other was flat on the counter top.

She heard nothing at first except the pounding of her heart and her harsh breaths. Then a slight scuff of his shoes on the floor. The fabric of his trousers rubbed against her bum cheeks before she felt the press of his hardness. His body covered hers as he leaned over her, pressing down on her so that she felt every contour of the hardness of his chest and abdominal muscles.

"So you want to push me? You want me to spank you. I watched you fuck my friend. Yet, you won't give me the benefit of the doubt for a girl whom I had sex with months ago. Joy was a one-night stand. She's the only person from Park Hotel that I've touched. I don't have a harem. I will never disrespect you like that."

His hot breath whispered on her skin. The pulse on her throat jumped as she swallowed.

"Okay," she whispered.

She felt his chest rise and fall as he sighed.

"You want me like this, don't you? Are you excited that I have you spread on the kitchen counter? You don't know if I'm going to fuck you or spank you." He pressed his hips against her and she felt his bulge, hard and heavy.

Please, fuck me. She begged silently.

He moved back and without warning, a palm descended on left bum cheek in a sharp hard thwack.

"Oh!" The cry left her in a shocked gasp as pain bloomed up her nerve endings. She didn't get time to breathe again before another hit on the same spot.

Shit. He wasn't taking it easy on her. The thwacks kept landing, alternating between the cheeks. Heat and pain flared, set her body ablaze. She gripped the edge of the counter, grinding her teeth, determined not to cry. But the pain got too much and tears built up in her eyeballs. She squeezed her eyes shut, panting, struggling to breathe.

His palm landed on a sore spot.

"Please," she cried out, tears spilled onto the wooden counter. She won't ever accuse him of spanking like a girl again.

He stopped, stepped away.

"Stay there," he instructed.

Breathing heavily, she couldn't even move. Her legs felt like jelly so she couldn't stand properly.

Her bum ached so she couldn't sit down anyway. The only thing holding her up was the counter she half lay across.

She heard sounds of movement. She was still trying to work through the fog of pain so she didn't understand what he was doing. It wasn't until she smelled the aroma that she realised he was cooking food.

While she was spread out half naked on the central island.

Chapter Eleven

Tope carried on with his activities—the steady thumps of knife slicing vegetable on the chopping board, the sizzle of onions on the frying pan and eventually, the rattling of the stainless steel lid on the pan as the contents bubbled. In all that time, he didn't say anything to her.

Anuli didn't dare move. Her ass still throbbed although not as painfully as when he'd been smacking it.

Of course, staying in place because a man had ordered her to do so went against the grain. Her instincts screamed for her to push off the counter and face him square on.

Still, her body felt weighted into place by the knowledge that she'd misbehaved and he'd disciplined her. This was her corner time. Icy heat spread through her limbs and chest, chilling her out.

She swallowed excessively, opening and closing her mouth, struggling to find the right words. Her chest tightened and her body became heavy. She'd never been so conflicted.

Guilt pelted her skin for the way she'd behaved towards Tope. She couldn't really explain the red mist that had hovered over her from the minute Joy had mentioned Tope's name. The burning sensation in her chest that had turned to a flash of anger when Tope had mentioned the woman's name.

She'd never been one to compare herself to other women and she wasn't naive enough to think that Tope hadn't been with others. But having one of those girls in her face, trying to run her down, and she'd lost it.

Her reaction to Tope had been reckless, irrational. She did have a habit of behaving irrationally when it concerned the people she cared about.

She'd been furious at Peter when he'd started dating Tessa because Tessa had been her best friend and her lover. It wasn't until after Peter had intervened and prevented Tessa from being suspended from college and missing out on her exams that Anuli had realised how much Peter loved Tessa. She'd had to back off and wish both of them well.

Those same feelings of anger had arisen today after her confrontation with Joy, this time directed at Tope. But surely, there wasn't more between her and him.

Yes, the sex was fantastic. And yes, he was a good man to the people around him. But that didn't mean she felt anything more for him than lust.

She'd never been in a relationship with anyone else other than Tessa. The two of them had clung together for survival because they'd needed each other.

The men had been fleeting sexual encounters that didn't mean anything more than a way to earn cash.

Anuli didn't know how to need anyone else. After Tessa moved on, she'd made up her mind to move on alone. She wasn't going to give herself to anyone else the way she'd been devoted to Tessa.

So what was it she had with Tope?

He was the first person outside Tessa who took the time to know her. Her attitude and behaviour didn't put him off. Her actions last week in Bosco's house hadn't stopped him. Neither had her actions today.

This terrified her.

He'd told her not to be afraid of him. But she was afraid.

He seemed to know her too well.

She became aware that he'd switched off the burners of the cooker. She heard the scuff of the high stool being pulled back and opened her eyes.

Tope settled on the stool by the island counter. A plate of jollof rice with grilled beef sat on the counter in front of him. He lifted a spoonful to his mouth, chewing with relish.

She braced her elbows, ready to push off. "Can I get up?"

He flicked his gaze to her face. "No."

"Oh, come on," she protested.

He put his fork down. "Do you even know what you did wrong tonight?"

She screwed up her face. "I shouted at you and threatened to stab you with a knife. I shouldn't have. I just snapped, thinking of you and that girl. I'm sorry."

He sighed. "Okay. Go and put a skirt on. I'll dish out some food for you."

"Thank you." With her palms on the cool counter, she got up slowly and walked stiffly into the bedroom. She found a jeans skirt from her bag and pulled it on.

When she returned to the kitchen, he'd laid a place next to him and another plate of steaming food sat on the counter. She went slowly and climbed onto the high stool.

She winced and shot off the hard chair. "Is it okay if I stand and eat?"

He nodded and didn't say anything else to her while they ate.

That night, he didn't touch her before or after they got into bed. This was the first time he didn't pull her into his arms while they were in bed. It was also the first night they didn't have sex since she'd been in his house.

On Saturday, they were both back at work. Joy wasn't on duty but none of the other women gave her any hassle. Her shift ended early as she'd been working all week.

She decided to pop into the local takeaway restaurant not far from the hotel. She sent a text to Tope to tell him where she'd gone, knowing he still had an hour or so before he finished. He always wanted to know where she was at all times. After yesterday, she didn't want any reason for them to quarrel.

She arrived at the restaurant, queued up and eventually got to the front of the counter. She ordered food to go for both her and Tope and sat down in a corner chair to wait for the order to be ready.

She was typing a message to Tessa on her phone when she heard a man's voice. "Hey you."

She looked up to find Telema George standing in front of her, fists shaking and neck muscles corded. The man had nearly raped Tessa and had falsely accused the other girl of theft. The man was an A-grade asshole.

Clenching her jaw, she counted out to five. The only reason she hadn't responded to his aggression was because she'd promised Tope she'd be on her best behaviour. So she ignored the man and carried on fiddling with her phone.

Telema leaned over her and grabbed her arm, his hold tight enough to hurt. "I'm talking to you. I know your friend's boyfriend has a hand in what happened to me."

"Let go of me, asshole," she snapped and stood up. She didn't know what the hell he was talking about but she didn't care.

"What did you call me?" His eyes bulged and sweat settled on his forehead, vein throbbing.

"You heard me." She braced her hands on her hips. "I know what you did to Tessa. If you think you can intimidate me, you're picking on the wrong person."

"Your friend is a slut and so are you. You shouldn't be seen in places like this."

"And you rape women," she said in a voice loud enough for people around to hear.

Somebody gasped before she felt the sting of a palm on her cheek. The impact of the slap sent her head jerking just as pain flared on her face. Black spots formed in the corners of her eyes. She swayed on her feet.

In her dizzy state, she barely noted Telema's sneer as he walked off.

"Madam, you have to leave." Another man stood before her, a security guard in the blue and black uniform.

Her ear was ringing from the slap and her brain struggled to process his words. She blinked several times, confused about what was going on. "I can't leave. I've already paid for the food."

"Show me your receipt," he said and she handed him the paper in her hand.

He walked to the counter. She thought he would bring her meal. Instead, he came back with cash. "Here's your money. Now leave."

She glanced around the place. Everyone was staring at her including Telema who was seated with a woman, still sneering. "This is not fair."

What did she do wrong? She'd never felt so humiliated. Not when she worked as a call girl. Those men didn't treat her badly.

Yet, she was in a takeaway restaurant full of so-called civilised people and they didn't care that she was a victim. She'd been assaulted and instead of helping her, they were kicking her out.

Angry tears burned the back of her eyes. She balled her hands into fists, took a deep breath and walked out with her head high. Outside, the heat of the sun hit her shoulders. The tears built up in her eyes but she refused to let them fall.

She was crossing the Park Hotel car park when Tope walked out towards her.

"I thought you went to buy some takeaway. Where is it?" he asked.

She shook her head as a huge lump sat in her throat. She didn't want to tell him what happened anyway. He would think she'd started the trouble.

He peered down at her and she averted her gaze. She swallowed the lump in her throat.

"Are you ready to go home?" she asked in a choked voice.

He gripped her shoulders, making her face him. "What happened? You don't look okay."

She shook her head again, closing her eyes.

"Tell me, damn it. What upset you?"

"It's Telema." She broke down and told him what happened.

He didn't say anything when she finished. Just took her hand and led her to his car. He waited for her to climb in. Then he got into the driver's seat and drove out of there with tyres squealing.

She squeezed her eyes shut, glad for the silence in the car aside from the humming of the cool air-conditioner.

The car stopped with a jerk, making her lurch forward although restrained by the seatbelt. Her eyelids flew open. They were in the car park of the restaurant.

"What are we doing here?" she asked in shock, glancing at Tope.

"Taking care of business," he answered ominously. "Stay in the car if you want to. I'll be back shortly."

Perhaps he just wanted to get the food she'd previously ordered. However, she didn't want to go in there. Didn't want to face those people again.

Tope shut the car door and strode into the restaurant. Would he really buy food from here now after what they did to her? Her misery increased. Surely, Tope wasn't that insensitive.

Her jaw clenched. She scrambled out of the car, determined to face the people and get Tope to return to the car without the food.

Her heart thumped hard against her ribs as she shoved the swinging glass door and entered the foyer. Her gaze darted around the spacing, searching for Tope. He wasn't at the counter. The area wasn't as busy as it had been earlier.

On the left edge of her vision, she noticed movement. A commotion. Turning fully, she saw Tope haul Telema to his feet by his right arm.

"What the hell are you doing?" Telema shouted as he struggled. "Let me go."

Tope didn't slow down and dragged him to the foyer where the security man intervened.

"Sir, let him go," the uniformed man said, his gaze darting between the two men.

"No, I won't. You were here when he assaulted a woman and no one helped her," Tope replied as he twisted Telema's arm at his back.

"You're hurting my hand," Telema cried, his face screwed up in pain, sweat glistening on his skin.

"Get on your knees," Tope ordered.

"What?" Telema grimaced, his Adam's apple bobbing again and again.

"Get on your goddamned knees and apologise to the woman you dared to slap," Tope tilted his head at Anuli who still stood by the entrance.

"I'm not kneeling for that wh—" Telema let out a long howl as Tope twisted his hands.

Anuli swore she heard bones snapping.

"You broke my finger!" Telema collapsed on his knees, clutching his right hand with his left. His little finger looked skewed, pointing in a different direction from the rest.

Ouch. Anuli gasped, turning away in shock. Tope had broken the man's fingers. For her. Adrenaline tingled through her body.

"Next time, you'll think twice before you hit a woman." Tope walked up to Anuli and took her hand. Then he led her to the counter. "I want to speak to the manager."

"Sure, sir," one of the servers responded before disappearing in a door at the back.

At the entrance, the woman who had been with Telema spoke on the phone as the security man helped Telema to his feet and out of the exit.

The server came back minutes later with a man in a white shirt and black trousers.

"How can I help you?" the man asked.

"My name is Tope Balogun. I'm the chief of security at Park Hotels. My fiancée came here earlier to buy some food and a man assaulted her in your restaurant. Instead of your staff helping her out, they sent her away without the food she came for. I'm very disappointed. We at Park Hotels have a good working relationship with your business as we refer a lot of our guests over here. But if this is how you treat women, then I'm going to advise our marketing manager to revise our policy of referrals."

"I'm sorry, sir. I was unaware that this woman was your fiancée." The man tugged at his shirt collar in jerky motions.

"It doesn't matter who she is. The important thing is that no one bothered to help her. It's frankly disgusting."

"I apologise totally and we will be revising out policy so that staff know to help in future. In the meantime, please feel free to order anything you want compliments of the restaurant."

"We will," Tope replied and led Anuli to a table. He waited for her to sit before pulling up the chair and sitting next to her.

A buzz still remained around them as people talked.

Anuli couldn't help gawking at Tope. The man kept surprising her. She couldn't get over the fact that he'd broken Telema's finger.

No man had fought in her corner before. No man.

A fluttering sensation filled her stomach and her pulse raced. She reached across and grabbed his hand as a smile bloomed across her face.

"Thank you," she said as she met his dark, intense gaze. Everyone in the room disappeared except for the two of them. "You know we don't have to stay here."

"We do. I need to prove a point to everyone around. No one hurts you and gets away with it. No one," he said it as a vow, bringing their joined hands up to his lips.

She leaned against his side, glad to have him here with her.

Tope was one hell of a man. She finally saw that.

Chapter Twelve

Anuli and Tope stayed at the restaurant to eat their meals but left soon afterwards. Throughout the meal, she maintained some kind of physical contact with him, whether it was just their thighs brushing together or her hand clasped in his.

Being tactile worked for her on so many levels, as a way to comfort her when she was upset as well as for pleasure.

This evening, holding onto Tope proved to be much more. She couldn't quite describe the way it made her feel except that she didn't want to lose the connection.

On the drive back to his place, she shifted and placed her head on his shoulder so that she could retain the link.

"Would you like to go out tonight?" Tope asked as they neared his house.

"Out? Where?" She lifted her head from his shoulder to stare at him, her face puckered.

He glanced at her. "I know you like to party at the weekends. So we can go to Xtasy or another club later."

"Oh." She hadn't thought about going clubbing tonight.

"What?"

"Honestly, I didn't think about it."

"Really?" He beamed a smile that lit up his face.

"Yeah. But if you want to go out, then that's fine."

He pulled up in front of his gates. "No. I don't mind. What would you like to do?"

"Is it okay if we just hang out tonight? You know, just chill, in your house?"

He jerked back, eyes widened. "Of course we can just chill."

He reached over and squeezed her hand before getting out to the open the gates. Then he was back and driving across the driveway into the car port.

She pushed the door and got out of the car. Pulling the left gate while he pulled the right one, she helped with locking up. After he secured the padlock, he placed his left arm across her shoulders like he'd done the first night he'd brought her here.

Today, she curled her right arm around his back as they walked to the front door.

"If I didn't know better, I'd say you like me," Tope said with a grin as he reached for the door knob. The keys clinked when he turned the lock.

She sucked in a deep breath and let it out in a sigh. "You wouldn't be wrong. After a week with you, I find myself liking you."

With a wide grin, he pushed the door open and waited for her to go in before following. "I'm happy that you like me."

There was still an hour or so before the sun went down, so they didn't need to turn on the lights. She walked ahead to the bedroom, dumped her bag on the bed and sat on it to take her shoes off.

Tope turned on the ceiling fan when he came in and the gently whirring sound was a kind of background noise as he sat on the armchair in the corner and toed his shoes off.

She rested her elbows on her thighs and leaned forward. "About last night. You didn't touch me...we didn't have sex."

His fingers paused on the button on his shirt. He lifted his gaze to meet hers. The corners of his eyes were pinched. He swallowed hard, his Adam's apple bobbing.

"I was upset." He rubbed his hand on the back of his neck.

"I guess it was because of what I did," she replied, her cheeks heating. She shifted, appalled at how she'd overreacted yesterday.

His chest rose and fell when he puffed out a heaving breath. "It was what you said rather than what you did. I was more worried about you hurting yourself with the knife than hurting me. I knew I could disarm you eventually."

He sighed again. "But what you said cut me deeper than a knife."

"Oh." She tried to recall what she'd said to him. She'd talked about her clash with Joy. She'd been rude, accused him of having a harem, told him to go to hell and taunted him about the spanking. Any of those things could upset anyone. "I really don't know what to say. I'm sorry."

"You told me you didn't care about me." He bent his head and scrubbed his hands over his scalp.

"After everything, I started questioning myself and wondering what was the point. If I would ever be able to convince you that this thing between us could be amazing if you let it become what it should be. I guess some of my hope died last night."

What had she done? Without thinking, she got off the bed and took the steps needed to cover the space separating them. She lowered herself onto her knees on the cool flooring. Then she lifted her hands to cover his on his head.

"I was lashing out yesterday. You need to know that I do that a lot." She decided to be honest with him about some of her feelings at least. It was only fair since he was being honest about his emotions. "I lash out verbally and physically when I'm upset. I also tend to want to go and be by myself when I'm upset. I shut people out. That's partly why I wanted to leave. I wanted to go and be by myself. But you achieved the same effect by making me have time out after the spanking. I used the time to think and calm down."

He lifted his head, his eyes gleaming. "Are you saying that the discipline works for you?"

Her lips tugged up in a half smile. "I really shouldn't admit it. Yes. The spanking helps to tone down my attitude which I need to work on. And the time out worked great too. Usually when I'm upset, I shut people out and end up alone. I find that I don't like being alone so I go partying, a mix of boozing and sex. It's reckless. And although I've been relatively lucky so far. I doubt my good fortune will continue forever where that's concerned. But with time out, I can still shut you out but I know I'm not alone."

"You never need to be alone."

"That's good. Because I hate being alone." She stroked her thumb over his lips. His tongue darted out and swiped it. Her breath hitched. "What can I do to make it up to you?"

"You can kiss it better."

"I sure can." She gave him a sexy smile as she lowered her hands to his belt buckle.

He chuckled, the deep sound doing naughty things to her. "That wasn't what I meant."

"I know, but it'll still help." She undid his fly.

He didn't protest as she reached in and pulled his throbbing dark erection out. She teased him with her fingers, sliding up and down over the smooth skin and pressing the vein running underside.

He let out a long, tortured groan, lifting his hips to push his trousers down.

She bent forward and took his cock in her mouth, letting his weight and girth fill her up. She let out a moan as precum coated her tongue and his taste exploded on her taste buds. At the same time, his masculine scent filled her nostrils. Arousal made her squirm as her pussy creamed.

She tongued the slit at the head of his dick. His head fell back and the sound of his explosive groan filled the room.

His hand settled on her hair. "Yes, suck my cock."

She sank her mouth down over him as the hand in her hair tightened. The pain made pleasure explode on every nerve ending, her insides pulsing along with her thumping heart.

She used her tongue to tease his skin and he shuddered, just as the grip on her hair tightened again, sending shockwaves through her body, both of pain and pleasure.

She moaned around his length, bobbing her head up and down, her nose almost grazing the short curly hairs at his groin.

"You look so fucking sexy on your knees. I don't think I'm going to last long." The words came out in gruff exhales as if he was about to lose it for real.

She wanted him to come, in her mouth. She wanted to drive him insane. Reaching between his thighs, she cupped his balls as she worked his shaft with the other hand. Then she leaned down and sucked one sac into her mouth.

"Fuuuccckkkk." He groaned, his body tensed.

Then she tongued the other ball of flesh while pumping his shaft. He trembled. He actually trembled. He had to be so close. She returned her mouth over his dick and sucked him deep.

He started thrusting his hips as he exhaled a long moan. His body spasmed as hot salty cum splashed on her tongue. It poured out continuously and she swallowed as much as she could. Some trickled down her chin. He kept thrusting until the cum stopped and he fell back into the chair, panting.

He surprised her when he leaned down, grabbed her arms and lifted her onto his lap. Then he kissed her, taking her breath away. He must have tasted himself on her. They broke apart, both of them panting.

"I've never met a woman who could do the things you just did with your tongue," he said in a still gruff voice as his hand slid between her thighs.

"I've got skills," she said and her breath hitched when he palmed her pussy.

"You sure have." His fingers slid under her panties. "And you're wet. You must love giving head."

"I like to be in control sometimes. Power is a great turn on." She wriggled as he circled her clit and stroked down to her slick slit.

"You're a switch." His left hand covered her breast, squeezing, kneading.

"What's—what's that?" Her brain struggled to follow the conversation now as it tried to focus on the pleasure zinging through her body.

"A switch is someone who alternates between being dominant and being submissive. While some people are one or the other, you can be both at different times."

She'd never actually thought about it like that but he summarised her accurately. With her female lovers, she liked to be the one in control. But with some men, especially Tope, she wanted to give him all the control during sex and even outside of sex.

He pinched her nipple and the arc of energy travelled straight to her clit. She canted her hip just as his fingers thrust inside her, his thumb pressed down on her hardened nub.

"Tope!" she screamed as her orgasm was ripped out of her. She collapsed onto him, heaving breaths gushing out of her.

He lifted her hip and then his cock was inside her, ramming into her. His lips claimed hers in a ravaging kiss. She ground against him as he thrust up. She gripped his shoulders as he held her down tight. All her senses honed in on him, her pleasure rising again. She wanted to hang on so that she could come again when he came. But soon, she was floating and he was grunting his release inside her.

She lowered her sweat-slicked face on his shoulder as she caught her breath. His ragged breath whooshed against her neck where he placed a tender kiss.

He rubbed his hand gently down her spine. "I'm sorry. I didn't use a condom. I just needed to be inside you so much, I didn't think."

She lifted her head and looked at him. He looked visibly distressed, as if he'd offended her. How could he offend her? She was the one who'd sold her body for a living. The one most likely to infect him with something. But she'd been tested recently and had the all clear.

"No. It's not your fault. I was the one who gave you BJ without using a condom. I broke my rule first." She stroked his face to reassure him.

"I'm clean. I promise you. We get tested at Park Hotels regularly as part of the employment contract. But you could still get pregnant."

She couldn't help the bark of laughter that escaped her. But there was no humour in it. Her chest tightened in pain. Her hands dropped from his face. She pushed off his body and crossed arms over her chest. "If that's what you're worried about, then you shouldn't be."

Tears burned the back of her eyes but she blinked to push them back.

"Are you on the pill or some other contraceptive?" He pulled his shirt over his head and tugged down his trousers.

She turned her back and shoved her skirt down, taking the rest of her clothes off. Then she got into the bed and curled into a ball. Her chest tightened again, hurting so badly.

"Hey, what's the matter?" The mattress sank as Tope got on the bed and lifted her into his arms.

"If I tell you that some people hurt me, what will you do?" she asked, her gaze staring at the far wall. It was time she told him the truth about her.

He cared about her. And she'd watched him break a man's finger today. But what she needed him to do for her would involve something worse. Something premeditated and cruel. Something without mercy.

"I will tell you to give me their names and I'll hunt them down and make each one of them pay," he said in a voice full of sincerity.

She didn't doubt that he would hurt anyone who hurt her. But that wasn't enough for her. "Would you kill for me?"

"Why? What's the matter?" His voice was deeper now. Concerned.

She turned around and met his gaze. "Please answer me. If I asked you to kill someone for me, would you do it?"

133

Chapter Thirteen

Tope's body froze as his heart thudded hard against his chest. Was Anuli testing him? Did she want him to prove his loyalty and commitment to her?

He'd already shown her earlier this evening that he wouldn't stand for anyone mistreating her. He'd meant it when he'd said no one would hurt her and get away with it.

The audible stress in her voice and the way she rocked back and forth showed her distress. Something bad had happened to her.

He drew in slow, steady breaths and spoke in a careful, controlled tone to suppress the anger threatening to boil over in his veins. Whoever caused her this much anguish would feel pain by his hands.

"Anuli, sure, I will kill to protect you. Do you want me to take a blood oath for you? Do you want me to prove that I would die first before I let anything bad happen to you?"

She shook her head slowly. "I know you would die for me, Tope. But I don't want your death. I want someone else to die."

He held her shoulders, not wanting to force her to speak but wanting to find out who she wanted dead. "Who is this person and why do you want him or her dead?"

The skin around her eyes bunched up and her hands clenched into fists. Her shoulders curled and it looked like she would crumple if he wasn't holding her upright.

Something tore at his heart, seeing her like this. She was his tiger. Not a frightened mouse. He really was going to kill someone, whoever did this to her.

In his line of work, he was there to protect people. Yes, he would kill to defend those he sheltered. But he'd never considered murder, premeditated cold-blooded killing, until just now. Until he saw the light die in the eyes of the woman he loved.

Because there was no doubt in his mind that he loved her. Had fallen for her from the first day he'd seen her eyeballing him in Peter's suite. Spending the last week with her had only confirmed what he'd known for months.

He'd always felt that he would know the woman he would spend the rest of his life with as soon as he met her. He'd been proven right. He would put a ring on her finger and swear to devote the rest of his life to her in the blink of an eye.

But he'd also known that there were demons that haunted her. He'd been waiting for her to open up to him so he could slay those demons for her.

"Anuli." He lifted her right hand and slowly unclenched the fingers before placing her open palm over the left side of his chest. His skin electrified on contact and he took shuddering breaths. "If someone hurt you and you want them dead, then you have my word that he or she is a dead person."

She exhaled a heavy breath and her shoulders relaxed as if a big weight had been lifted from her. Her eyes glassed over. Tears pooled and dropped onto her cheeks.

"You don't know what those words mean to me." Her voice was low and strained.

He stroked his thumb across her cheek, flicking the wetness away. "You are my beating heart. I will do anything for you."

"I realise that." She swallowed. "The gun I bought wasn't to defend myself. I want to use it to kill my stepfather when I find him."

His grip on her hand tightened but he didn't say anything, wanting her to talk at her own pace.

She placed her head against his chest and spoke in a monotone voice that was devoid of any emotions, as if she wanted to distance herself from what she was saying.

"I think I was two years old when my father died. Apparently, my mother had gotten pregnant very young and she wasn't married to him at the time. Her parents had kicked her out. She'd gone to stay with my father's family. My father's family had reluctantly paid bride price. But when my father died, they kicked my mother out. They hadn't wanted their son to marry her anyway so there was no reason for her to stay, especially since I wasn't a boy."

Fuck. Tope growled and tightened his grip around Anuli, giving her a squeeze. This issue of the way girl children were treated as second class humans annoyed him to no end. He made a mental list of people to find and hurt. Anuli's paternal and maternal families were on that list.

"My mum tried her best to take care of me. I really don't remember much apart from the things she told me. A man started showing up where we lived. He would bring gifts for her and for me. He was very nice to us. When he asked my mum to marry him, she said yes. I was probably seven or eight at the time. She thought he would take care of us. To be honest, he did for a while. We lived in a nice house. I even had my own room instead of sharing my mother's bed like I'd done when it was just me and my mum in a one-room apartment."

She stopped talking, her breath becoming a little ragged as if she struggled to breathe.

"Just take your time," he said in a soothing tone as he massaged her back with light, gentle strokes.

Her breathing levelled out eventually as she relaxed again.

"Things changed when he started coming into my bedroom at night. At first, he would just touch me inappropriately as he supposedly settled me into bed. It wasn't until he did more and forced himself into me that I told my mum because it hurt so much. My mum was out, working late at a restaurant. I cried so much but he told me not to say anything, that it was our secret. My mum eventually found out the next day when she saw blood in my pants that she was washing and asked to see. I had to tell her what my stepfather did. She packed up our things and confronted him that night. They argued. She left him and took me with her. We didn't get very far. She was run over by a hit and run driver."

Wetness splattered on his chest and he knew she was crying although she didn't sob. Tope couldn't explain the mix of emotions taking a tumble inside him. Rage, anguish and sadness at all the things she'd gone through as a young child.

Murder actually seemed an easy option considering what her stepfather had done. He would cut the man open and make him die a slow, painful death.

He held onto Anuli, letting her know by the way he held and stroked her that he would always be here for her, that he would never let her endure anything that bad again.

She sniffled a few times before speaking again. "I can never forget the image of that car going over my mother's body, or the sickening thud and crunch of her body as her life was crushed out. I didn't see the driver, just knew it was a dark-coloured car. I sat beside my mother's body. People gathered, even my stepfather turned up. We weren't far from his house. The police got involved. They took my mother to the morgue. My stepfather took me back to his house. He played the role of grieving husband until my mother was buried. In all this, even the police didn't bother to ask me what me and my mother were doing on the road so late at night with luggage."

The hand that she had on his chest curled into a fist. "The thing is, my stepfather is a policeman. So he was a man of authority. No one ever questioned

whatever story he told them about that night.
Never mind that I was a witness to what happened
in the house as well as on the road. Of course, the
sexual abuse continued. My stepfather told me he'd
killed my mother and that he would kill me too if I
ever told anyone about what was happening to me.
It wasn't just him. He'd take me to men's houses
and leave me there for them to do whatever they
wanted. It was as if I was a bribe or gift or
something. Honestly, I wanted to die. I was going
to kill myself. I had everything planned out. But
one day, he took me to this big house. Really nice
house. And I met a girl who was only a few years
younger than me. I saw my pain reflected in her
eyes. I knew she was going through the same things
I was so I couldn't kill myself and leave her to suffer
alone. That girl was Tessa. We became friends and
years later when the opportunity came, we ran
away together."

When she finished talking, she lay silently in his
arms. He didn't move, just held her tight.

He knew Peter had commissioned an
investigation into Tessa's and Anuli's past. But
Tope hadn't known the sickening depth of what
those men had done. He certainly knew that he
wouldn't sit around to wait for the men to be
arraigned to court and face trial. They would be
getting justice by his hand.

"I'm going to kill your stepfather and any man
involved in his paedophile ring," he vowed to her.

"Thank you," she muttered against her chest.
She sounded drowsy. Soon enough, he heard the

steady rhythm of her breathing, indicating she'd fallen asleep.

He waited until she settled. Then placed her back on the mattress and covered her up with a sheet.

It was dark now so he scrambled to pull his trousers back on. He pulled his phone out, walked to the door and shut it behind him before navigating in the dark to the kitchen. He turned on the light, walked to the fridge and took out a bottle of water.

He flicked to the contacts on his phone and pressed to call Bosco's number. He needed help to formulate a plan of action and he trusted Bosco with his life. The man they were going to take down was a high ranking member of the police force. A man who should protect the vulnerable and yet used his position of authority to abuse others.

Bosco picked up the phone. "Hey, man. What's up?"

Tope scrubbed a hand over his head. "Can you come over?"

The way he felt, he couldn't talk on the phone.

Bosco must have detected something in his voice. "Sure. Give me a few minutes."

"Okay." Tope switched off his phone, placed it on the counter and scrubbed both hands over his face. Then he poured himself the cool water and drank from the glass.

He put the bottle back in the fridge and went to sit on the veranda. The security lights lit up the place. He tried to sort through his emotions. The overriding one was rage. But he knew he had to put a lid on it for Anuli's sake. Losing his temper would do no good. Anyway, the persons he was angry at were not close by for him to vent on them.

He heard the sound of Bosco's motorbike as it pulled up outside his gate and hurried to open it. Bosco rode in and parked besides Tope's SUV under the car port. Tope locked the gates again.

"What's going on?" his friend asked, his helmet hooked onto the handlebar of his Suzuki power bike.

Tope squeezed his hands, the bunch of keys digging into his skin as he paced back and forth. "Anuli just told me some fucked up shit from her past. Some asshole abused her as a child. I want to kill him. In fact, I'm going to kill him."

Bosco didn't look shocked as he met his gaze. The man had seen some crazy stuff in his time. Nothing fazed him these days. Bosco nodded his head. "Come indoors."

Tope followed his friend back into the house. It was better to talk in here rather than outside in case someone was eavesdropping, which was likely to happen in a neighbourhood where everyone knew everyone's business.

Bosco took bottles of Guinness out of the fridge. The two of them sat in the living room while he summarised what had happened to Anuli and they made plans. By the time they each crashed on individual sofas in the early hours of the morning, they had a plan of action in place and a list of those to recruit to help them carry out an abduction and assassination.

Chapter Fourteen

Sunlight beamed in through the curtained windows as Anuli peeled her eyes open. She stretched, her body tingling as she remembered last night with Tope on the chair. She turned around expecting to find him beside her. He wasn't.

Perhaps he was making breakfast. Last Sunday, he'd made breakfast while she'd still been asleep. A smile curled her lips as the memories flooded her mind.

So much had happened since he'd first brought her here as his captive. At that time, all she'd wanted to do was to go back to the one-room studio she lived in.

Now she swung her legs over the side of the low wooden frame bed. The whirring fan spun overhead. Thankfully, there wasn't a power cut. She found one of Tope's T-shirts and pulled it over her head. She loved the faint scent of him on her skin.

She padded out of the room, her bare feet slapping against the cool hard flooring. She peeped into the kitchen first but there was no one in there and no sign of any cooking in progress. Wondering where Tope was, she headed to the living room and stopped as soon as she crossed the threshold.

143

She saw Tope first. He lay across the sofa by the
left wall, wearing the pair of trousers he'd worn
yesterday but no shirt. His dark chest rose and fell
with the rhythm of his breathing as he slept. Four
opened bottles of Guinness lay on the low dark
wood coffee table along with two used tall glasses.

Had he had a guest last night? He'd been
drinking with someone.

She tiptoed into the room, not wanting to wake
him in case he'd slept late. Her heart jolted in her
chest as she saw the other man lying across the
second adjacent sofa. Bosco.

She hadn't seen him at first because the sofa
backed the door and the dining area. She only saw
him when she stepped between the gap separating
the sofa and the wall with the entertainment unit.

The man was in a plain cotton navy T-shirt and
stone-washed jeans. His feet were bare, but a pair of
brown leather boots stood adjacent to the sofa. She
remembered him naked on his bed last Saturday
and warmth spread through her.

Bending down, she picked up the bottles gently
so they didn't clink loudly to wake the men as she
cleared the table. She balanced the items with her
fingers, stuffing some under her arms as she
returned to the kitchen. She tossed the empty
bottles back in the crate. When the crate was full of
empties, it would be returned to the store when
Tope wanted to buy a new crate of beer. She placed
the glasses in the sink and washed them absently.

Bosco was here? Why? It had to be because of
her, because of what she'd told Tope last night.

144

The first brick in the wall she'd built around herself had taken a tumble when Tope had told her about what he was doing for Mama Ejima and her kids. Men like him were rare to find.

She'd relaxed in his company, actually enjoying spending time with him, until her bust up with Joy at work, and her eventual aggression towards Tope. That had been the low point of the week.

She hadn't thought that anything could ruffle him until he had confessed that her words had hurt him badly. It was then she knew that beneath the hard shell everyone saw, Tope was a tender teddy bear where she was concerned. And to those he cared about like Mama Ejima and co.

Of course, his toughness came back to the fore after the incident with Telema. By breaking the man's fingers, Tope put himself in danger of arrest. He could get in trouble, all because of her.

She'd had no option but to tell him about her horrible childhood and the reason she'd bought a gun. He'd deserved to know.

Then he'd vowed to kill Uncle Joe and the men who'd abused her.

She believed him, had no reason to doubt him. His response had floored her.

The rest of the bricks around her heart crumbled as she realised there was another impenetrable shell protecting her now. Tope.

All the weight she'd carried for the past fifteen years lifted. For the first time in years, she'd slept all night long without waking once, without the ghost of her past lurking in the shadows.

She picked a tuber of yam from the cool larder. Placing it on the board on the counter, she sliced it into one and half centimetre wide discs. Then she peeled off the brown skins and cut the discs in two so they formed half moons. Once done, she placed the yam slices into a white plastic bowl, ran water from the tap into the bowl and washed the yam. Then she transferred the clean slices into a pan and filled it with water. She placed the pan on the hob, lit the flame underneath, added some salt to the pan and covered it to cook.

Tope said he liked having yam and eggs for Sunday brunch so she thought he'd appreciate it if it was ready when he woke up.

She scooped the yam peel and pressed the lever at the base of the bin with her foot. The lid popped open and she tossed the stuff in her hand in. Turning, she grabbed the cloth and wiped down the counter.

A prickling sensation made her glance back. Bosco leaned against the door post, his hooded eyes watching. His lips curled into a half-smile

Her heart rammed her ribs. How long had he been watching her?

"Hi." Her voice came out squeaky and she swallowed the lump in her throat.

"Morning," his deep voice rumbled and the smile widened, showing white teeth. He straightened and walked into the kitchen, his movement fluid. "How are you?"

She'd forgotten that animal magic he oozed from the first moment she'd seen him that had made her ride his cock shamelessly in Tope's presence. What was wrong with her?

Turning away, she swallowed. "I'm fine."

She momentarily forgot what she was supposed to be doing. She tugged at the T-shirt, her palms became sweaty. Why was it suddenly so hot in the kitchen?

Bosco walked to the fridge which was on the other side of where she stood. They had the central unit separating them, thankfully.

"Good," he said. She heard the sound of him pulling something out of the fridge. "Tope told me about your stepfather. I want you to know that we're going to end him and his sick network. Every one of them."

He spoke with such vehemence. She whirled around, a frown on her face. Why did he care? "You are?"

"Yes. Your stepfather doesn't deserve to live. But he's not going to have an easy death either. We're going to make sure of it." He came around with the bottle of water and grabbed one of the glasses Anuli had washed earlier from the sink drainer.

"I appreciate it. Thank you. But you sound as angry as Tope did last night. I understand why he'd be angry. But why do you care so much?"

He swallowed all the water from the glass and put it back in the sink before he answered. "Tope and I are brothers in arms. You're his girl. Anything that affects you affects him. And anything that affects him, affects me. It's that simple. Anyway, I think you're cool." He smiled again.

"And that's a compliment from Bosco."

At the sound of Tope's deep voice, Anuli whirled around to find him striding into the kitchen. Her heart raced as he pulled her into his arms and kissed her.

"Morning, Tiger. How are you feeling?" he asked, his large hands on either side of her face, his callused thumbs grazing her cheeks.

"I'm fine. I'm just making breakfast." She turned around, taking a deep breath. She picked up an onion as distraction.

Having both men in such close proximity made her feel as if she would melt and turn into a puddle on the floor. The temperature seemed to have gone up another notch. Perspiration dripped down her neck and trailed between her breasts. Her nipples tightened, chaffing against the shirt.

Tope stood behind her, his arms wrapped around her midriff, his lips grazing her left ear.

"You shouldn't have bothered. I was going to make breakfast." His warm breath whispered across her skin.

Bosco leaned against the counter, watching them. He'd assumed the relaxed pose she'd seen last weekend, his arms crossed over his chest, his eyes filled with amusement like he enjoyed watching her interact with Tope.

"It's okay. You guys were sleeping. It seemed you'd had a long night so I thought I'd make the food ready for when you woke up."

A hard bulge nudged her backside as Tope's fingers grazed the underside of her breasts. "Do you mind if Bosco joins us for breakfast?"

"Erm, no. Of course I'm cooking for all of us," she replied in a shaky, halting tone.

Her body shook from the hidden meaning in his words. It was as if he was asking permission for his friend to eat more than food. But that had to be ridiculous. She was the one allowing her brain to misinterpret his words.

"Bosco, please open the back door. It's a little hot in here." She breathed deeply. The window was open but the kitchen suddenly didn't seem big enough for the three of them. She felt as if she was being tormented by both men, as if they were pushing her to see what she would do. Her heart was racing and her skin prickled.

Bosco opened the door and she was glad for the cool air that rushed in.

"Do you need help with anything?" Bosco asked.

"No. I've got it all under control." She hoped she did. "You guys should go and relax. I'll let you know when the food is ready."

"Okay." Tope swept her ponytail aside, pressed a kiss to her shoulder and swatted her bum.

She yelped. He chuckled before releasing her and heading for the door.

Bosco winked at her and headed in the same direction as his friend. When both men had disappeared down the hallway, Anuli leaned against the counter and exhaled in relief.

She managed to give the food her full concentration and finished with the preparation. She set the dining table for three and transferred the food out in the lidded clear, glass dishes, putting everything on an aluminium tray before taking them into the living room.

When everything was ready, Tope and Bosco joined her at the table. Tope sat in his usual spot at the head. She sat to the right of him and Bosco to his left.

They ate and chatted easily. She found that Bosco was similar to Tope although he was very laid back.

"Bosco, do you have a girlfriend?" she blurted out halfway through the meal.

Bosco's smile froze for the briefest moment and then he was grinning again. "No. Do you have a friend you want to hook me up with?"

She laughed. "No. I was just wondering. A man like you must be popular with the ladies."

Bosco just chuckled.

Tope glanced from his friend to her, a lopsided grin on his face. "You're right. The girls all fall for him especially with his bike. But they don't realise he's not for settling down."

"You can't cage the wind, babe." Bosco winked at her.

"The wind, eh." She laughed. She'd once thought she'd never consider a serious relationship with a man. Yet here she was, sitting next to a man who meant more to her than any other. "There are factors that can affect the wind. I'm sure when the right woman comes along, you will think differently."

"She has you there, my man," Tope said, placing his fork on his empty plate.

"So are you guys going to tell me the plan?" she asked, wanting to discuss the topic neither of them seemed eager to broach.

Tope and Bosco looked at each and did the silent communicating thing again.

"Come on, guys. I know the reason Bosco is here is because you are making plans about my stepfather. I should know some if not all of it, don't you think?"

Bosco leaned back in his chair, glass half-filled with water in his right hand, left hand on the top of the adjoining chair.

Tope braced his elbows on the table, fingers steeped. "Yes, we're making plans about your stepfather. The plan is to grab him and take him to a secure location where we will extract the information about what he's done from him and get him to name his accomplices. Of course, because he's a prominent member of the Nigerian Police Force, it won't be easy to do that. So we need to mount surveillance on him as well as find a secure location out of state to hold him until we're done with him. I'm sorting out the surveillance and Bosco is dealing with the safe house."

He reached out and covered her hand with his. "That's all you need to know for now. You don't need me to tell you that no one else can know about our plans."

"Of course. I know." She would never share this with anyone else. What Tope and Bosco were planning could get them into trouble, all because of her. "I want to see my stepfather after you finish with him."

She wanted to put a bullet through the man's head.

"Are you sure?" Bosco asked, his face puckered in a frown. "He's not going to be in a good state when we're done with him. He's going to be tortured."

"I know. I want you to torture him. After what that man did to me, he doesn't deserve anything less. But I want to put a bullet into him for killing my mother." Her voice tightened with anger.

Tope tugged her hand and pulled her up. She went across and sat on his lap. He wrapped his arms around her. "If that's what you want, then so be it."

Chapter Fifteen

Bosco stayed with them for the next few days. They'd agree to get their plan completed before Anuli had to go back to a new school year session in a few weeks.

She and Tope went to work daily as usual. At night, Bosco turned up and the men plotted. She saw them poring over physical maps spread out on the low table as well as the digital ones provided by Google on Tope's laptop. Aside from the general Atlas world maps they'd studied in school, she hadn't even known there were detailed geographical maps for each Nigerian state.

The men didn't involve her in the details of their plans. It made her appreciate that she would never have accomplished what she'd wanted to do without help. Without *their* help.

When she analysed her plans, she realised how flawed it had been. From what she'd found out through Peter, Joseph Uwadiegwu was the new Assistant Commissioner for Police, State Criminal Investigation department in Benue State. He had remarried and there was a young child but she wasn't sure if the boy was his or a stepchild like she'd been. Uncle Joe was a predator. Anuli would bet his wife had been a vulnerable woman when he'd met her and he'd taken advantage. She would also bet that the child wasn't his, which would indicate that the man had a pattern like any other sociopath.

Anuli had planned to travel up to Makurdi and wangle her way in to see him. She would've pretended as if she'd missed him so much and she'd wanted to see him. Once he'd relaxed enough in her company, she would have shot him. She would've confessed to his wife what Uncle Joe had done to her years ago and hopefully the woman would realise she'd saved her and her son.

Of course, that wasn't going to happen now. Anuli felt relief that she wasn't doing this alone. But she also felt fear on behalf of the men who had taken up this mission.

On Monday night, a man turned up at Tope's house. Siki. Anuli recognised him as one of the men who worked at Park Hotel's security. They'd already had dinner before the man arrived. She left the three men in the living room and went to the kitchen to wash up. Her phone beeped as she wiped down the counter. She picked it up from the central unit. It was a message on Whatsapp from her friend. She read the message as she left the kitchen, heading for the bedroom.

Tessa: Nuli, How now?

Smiling, Anuli sat on the bed before she typed a reply.

Anuli: Babe, I dey. How you?

Tessa: I've got news. We set a wedding date. It's in six months.

Anuli: Wow. Congratulations! I'm so happy for you. *dancing emoji*

Tessa: Thank you. I'm so happy. *smiling, laughing, dancing emojis*

Anuli: We will party like it is 1999. *Champagne emoji*

Tessa: Absolutely. Will you be my chief bridesmaid?

Anuli: *Grinning emoji* Yes! Yes! Yes! I feel like you just proposed to me.

Tessa: Crazy woman. So you have to come to Enugu and get involved with the planning. Erica, Peter's sister is a bridesmaid and helping me. But I need you.

Anuli: Babe, I can't come to Enugu at the moment.

Tessa: Oh, come on. What can be more important than hanging out with your BFF?

Anuli could never tell Tessa what was going on for obvious reason. But she settled for telling her half of the truth.

Anuli: There's someone. We've been hanging out a lot.

Tessa: Really? Wow. Guy or girl?

Anuli smiled. Tessa knew her so well. She could swing either way.

Anuli: Guy.

Tessa: So gist me now. Who is he? How long have you known him? Come on.

Anuli: You remember Tope, right?

Tessa: Tope? Which Tope?

Anuli: You know, from Park Hotel.

Tessa: OMG!!!!! That Tope. Big, scary, I-chew-nails-for-breakfast Tope.

155

Anuli: *Three laughing emojis* Yes, that Tope.

Tessa: You are one crazy woman. The guy scared the crap out of me the first day I saw him. I thought he was going to lock you up in the guard house.

Anuli laughed and shifted up in the bed so her back was against the headboard as she leaned on a pillow.

Anuli: *laughing emojis* You know me. I do some crazy shit.

Tessa: Yeah. Trust you to pick the biggest, baddest guy around.

If only Tessa knew that she hadn't picked Tope. Tope had picked her, determined not to let her go. If only Tessa knew there were three bad-ass men currently in the same house with her, she would freak out.

Tessa: Seriously though. Is he good to you?

Anuli: Yes. He's good. Not in the Peter sweet kind of way. You know. If I had a man like Peter, I would probably give him stroke or heart attack.

Tessa: Abeg, leave my sweet Peter out of it. I love him like that. *smiling emojis*

Anuli: I know you do. But I was just making a point about Tope. Tope is a good man, there's no doubt that he cares about me. But he is also as tough as steel. I need a man like him. I need his rigid strength. Otherwise he would crumble under the weight of the shit garbage I carry with me.

Tessa: *sigh* I understand. You seem happy and that's what's important to me.

Anuli: I am happy.

She was surprised to type those words but they were true. Heat radiated across her chest and she felt weightless whenever she thought about Tope.

Tessa: Good.

Anuli: Great. So I'll see you in a few weeks when you come back to PHC for registration.

Tessa: Oops. I forgot to tell you. I'm sorry.

Anuli: What?

Tessa: I got a place to study for a BA in French and German Languages at University of Nigeria, Nsukka.

Anuli: Wow. You didn't tell me you were applying to change schools.

Tessa: I'm sorry. I decided to change schools because I didn't want to go back to UniPort especially after what happened with Telema. I wasn't sure I was going to get the place at UNN so I waited until it was confirmed before telling you.

Anuli sighed. She couldn't hold it against her. After all, she was keeping secrets from her friend too.

Anuli: I understand. I'm happy you got a place. Now you can make a fresh start and be closer to Peter too.

Tessa: Thank you. Gotta go. Chat soon.

Anuli: Take care.

Anuli placed her phone on the bedside unit as the realisation dawned that she was losing her closest friend and companion. The move to UNN would be good for Tessa. But it meant Anuli would lose her confidante. She'd thought that when Tessa returned to Port Harcourt for the new school semester, they would live together as they'd done previously. Now, that wasn't going to happen. Her chest hurt and she rubbed a palm over it.

She got off the bed and walked to the living room. The men looked up when she walked in. It seemed Siki had left. Bosco and Tope sat together on the sofa, hunched over the laptop and chatting in low voices.

She ignored them and walked to the sideboard by the dining table. This was where Tope kept the hard liquor. She needed something stronger than beer.

She opened the cupboard and took out a bottle of whisky.

"Are you okay?" It was Bosco's voice.

She glanced in his direction. "I'm fine," she said in a sharp voice.

Tope looked up, a frown marring his expression. "What's going on?"

"What is this? A thousand and one questions? I want a drink and I'm going to have one." She took the bottle of whisky and walked out.

Behind her, scuffing sounds and then footsteps indicated that one or both men had followed her. She ignored them and walked into the kitchen, heading for the cupboard with the glasses.

Placing the whisky bottle on the counter, she reached up and took a short square-shaped tumbler out. She placed it on the counter just as Tope strode in.

"What's wrong?" he asked, heading in her direction.

Her grip on the glass tightened and she snapped. "Can a girl not have a drink around here without being interrogated?"

"Hey, watch the attitude." Tope placed his hand on her nape in a firm grip, reminding her of his authority.

She sucked in a deep breath, still annoyed but unwilling to incur his wrath at the moment. "I'm sorry. I just want to have a drink in peace."

His grip tightened for a few seconds, before relaxing. "Okay. It's been a stressful few days and we could all use a drink. Grab some more glasses."

She would rather drink alone but she couldn't argue with him. So she did as he instructed. He took the bottle of whisky and waited for her. She used her fingers to grip the three glasses together.

He kept his hand on her nape as they returned to the living room. He guided her to the sofa. She lowered the glasses onto the coffee table as she sat down. Tope sat beside her. He gave her neck one last squeeze before he released her to open the bottle of whisky.

Anuli chanced a stare in Bosco's direction who sat on the adjacent sofa. She couldn't read his expression as he shut the laptop. She puffed out another breath and sat stiffly.

Tope poured some of the amber liquid into the three tumblers. Without any words being exchanged, he took one. Bosco reached across and took the second glass.

The men didn't drink, just held on to the glasses as if waiting for her. She didn't know why she hesitated to reach for the remaining glass. She gripped her hands together and glanced at Tope.

He wore an indecipherable expression too. "Take the drink."

She snatched the glass and downed the drink. It burned her throat and chest. She sucked in a harsh breath and reached for the bottle. She expected Tope to stop her. He didn't.

The men were sipping their drinks as she poured a generous shot. She replaced the bottle on the table and this time took a gentle sip. The alcohol was already buzzing along her veins. She needed to pace herself so she wasn't sick.

"Tell me what happened." Tope's voice was gentle this time.

Anuli took another sip, allowed the burn to rip through her chest. "I've lost my best friend."

"What do you mean?" Bosco asked as he placed his glass on the table.

Anuli's grip on the glass tightened. "Tessa is not coming back to Port Harcourt. She got admission to do a programme at UNN."

"And that's bad?" Tope asked in a confused voice.

She scrubbed her left hand over her face. "Do you realise that the two of us have known each other for ten years? We've spent most of that time together. Now I don't know the next time I'll see her."

She slammed the glass on the table, sloshing amber liquid over the top.

"You knew she was getting married and would move in with Peter permanently." Tope was being reasonable.

But he only annoyed her more. She pushed off the sofa and paced to the window before turning back.

"Yes, I'm not stupid. I knew she would move in with him. But I thought I still had another three or four years with her at Uni. I thought she'd be back in a few weeks and we'd be sharing student digs." She balled her hands into fists. "She didn't even fucking tell me she was applying to UNN."

"Just the same way you didn't tell her you bought a gun or that you want to kill your stepfather."

He had a point but her fury only rose. She grabbed her drink, downed it. "It's not the same fucking thing."

Bosco shot off the sofa and grabbed her arm, preventing her from pacing.

"Calm down." He pried the glass off her tightened fingers.

She glared at Tope whose eyes were dark as the night and hard as granite. Then she turned her attention to Bosco. "Don't you understand that it's not the same thing? I can't tell her about Uncle Joe because I want to protect her. She's better off not knowing. What good would it do her to know? Tell me."

"None," Bosco said, his fingers rubbing her shoulder in a soothing manner. "She's better off not knowing our plans. Perhaps she thought she was protecting you by not telling you about her plans to change school. It must have been difficult for her to make the decision, knowing she would leave you here on your own."

She sighed. His hands on her body were doing more than just soothing her anger. A new sensation swirled around her as she inhaled his scent. Arousal. "I suppose so. Anyway, this is the reason I don't do relationships."

She shook off Bosco's hands and returned to the sofa. "Everyone leaves. My mother died and left me. Tessa left me to marry Peter. You—" she waved at Bosco who settled back on the sofa. "You're going to get on that your big motorbike and ride off into the sunset without me."

Bosco didn't dispute her words.

She turned to Tope who sat with his elbows on his knees and drink in his right hand. "And you, Tope. You're going to leave me too. One day, you'll realise that I'm just too damned screwed up for anyone to live with. But you know what, I'm not going to sit around and wait for that. I'm going to leave when I'm good and ready. I'm better off on my own."

Tope slammed his glass on the table before hands lifted her off the sofa, and then Tope's lips were crushing hers.

His grip, his mouth—everything overpowered her body, her senses. She couldn't move. Could only succumb to the fire that he lit in her veins. Her body heated, her skin prickled. She moaned, crying out into him as his tongue ravaged every corner of her mouth. She tasted him, his whisky, and the wild fierceness that was only Tope.

But she wanted more.

He broke the kiss, the two of them panting hard. His hand in her hair gripped so tight, she couldn't move it unless she wanted him to rip her hair off.

There was a wild glint in his eyes that she'd never seen before as she stared into the dark depths of his eyes.

"Tiger, listen to me. I'm disappointed that after all this time with me, you seem to have learned little about me. You should ask yourself 'What kind of man agrees to kill another for you? What kind of man will commit murder for you?'" He paused, letting the words sink into her.

"When you think about it—" he tapped his temple with his left index finger. "You should realise that I won't make that kind of sacrifice for just anyone. I am not like Peter. We are not in a conventional relationship like your friend has with her fiancé."

He shook his head.

"I love you. There's no doubt in my mind. But what I feel for you is more than love. Call it an obsession, if you like. It is what it is. But it also means you will never get the choice to leave me, just as I will never contemplate leaving you. Others may come and go but you and I are bound for life. Do you understand?"

She stared into his face. She should've been scared by the ferociousness of his words. Instead, it fired an uncontrollable emotion. The constriction in her chest loosened. She'd found a place, a man, to call home. She gripped his shoulders, digging her nails into his flesh.

"I understand. Death is the only thing that can separate us," she said in a surprisingly even voice.

"Exactly. So unless you're planning to kill me, I don't want to hear any more about you leaving." His grip on her hair tightened.

"Okay," she said in a breathless voice.

"Now, tell me what I can do to take away your pain. What can I do to make you feel better?" His grip on her hair loosened as his eyes softened.

She gulped in air and glanced at Bosco. He had the hooded expression. The one that made her heart skip a beat. Every inch of her skin prickled, making her feel as if she'd caught fire.

She swallowed and licked her lower lip. "I want you."

"You have me, always." Tope's thumb grazed behind her earlobe, adding to the tingling all over her body.

"I know. But..." She licked her lips again as sweat trickled down her back. "I want Bosco too."

"You do?" Tope shared a look with Bosco.

She hated that she could never understand their silent conversations. At least Tope didn't seem angry about what she was saying. This bolstered her.

"Yes, I want both of you to fuck me."

Chapter Sixteen

Neither Tope nor Bosco said anything. She glanced from one to the other, trying to decipher if they felt outrage after her announcement. Time slowed—seconds seemed like hours. All she could hear was the whoosh...whoosh sound of rushing blood in her ears.

She'd done it now. Pushed too far. Why couldn't she understand that other people had boundaries, even if she seemed to lack any?

Another track of perspiration travelled down her spine. She shivered as her body swung from hot to cold.

"Say something." Her voice was husky, her throat dry. She needed another drink. Tope's left hand was in her hair, his right on her hip as she straddled his lap, which prevented her from reaching for the drink on the table. "Did I ask for too much?"

"No, you didn't. We just want to be sure this is what you want—Bosco and I with you at the same time."

"Yes." The word rushed out of her as she expelled a breath of relief. "I want you both. I know it's a lot to ask. I can't get him out of my mind but I don't want to cheat on you."

Tope let out a huge breath, eyes going upwards. When he met her gaze, his eyes were shining as they locked onto hers. "You don't know what it means to me, us, to hear you say that."

She raised one brow and turned her gaze to Bosco. He was slumped against the sofa, a slow smile building on his lips and a palm over his heart.

"You just made my day," Bosco said with shaky laughter.

"I did?" These men were confusing her. This wasn't exactly the reaction she'd expected from telling two very macho men that she wanted both of them. They looked happy, as if her words had eased their concerns.

"Yes. I thought you were never going to ask for us, together," Bosco said.

"He'd almost given up hope. I expected you to jump his bones on Sunday, the way you were so turned on." Tope was grinning now.

She gasped. "You knew about that."

Bosco chuckled. "Yes. You were giving me that look. The one that makes my cock so hard it could drill through concrete. The pulse on your collar was thumping so hard and I could see the sweat trickling down your skin as it's doing now. Of course, when you asked me to open the back door, it was all I could do not to throw caution to the wind and fuck you right there. But I had to wait until you asked for me, for us."

Tope stroked down her temple. "We would never impose this on you. It has to be what you want."

These men were blowing her mind and yet all they were doing was talking to her. Did she fall asleep and dream this fantasy?

"Hang on, guys." She leaned back so she could see both of them at the same time. "So you're telling me that you're both happy to share me."

"I wouldn't use the word 'share' because it implies that he gets half of you and I get half, which isn't what this is about. This is about having the whole of you all the time. You have us and we have you. This is a fusion, a union of three."

Her heart jolted. What he was talking about sounded permanent. She hadn't thought beyond sex. Beyond this moment with the both of them.

"Are you saying that you want this...arrangement to carry on forever?"

Tope shrugged. "You and me, we're the core of this union. No matter what happens, we're not going to change. As for the trifecta, Bosco cares about you. But he's also a man who needs to fly free sometimes. You have to understand that about him."

She'd sensed that about Bosco from the moment she'd met him. He was a free spirit. A sudden lightness swept through her. She would always have Tope no matter what happened. This gave her the reassurance she needed after finding out about Tessa not coming back to PHC.

"Okay. Do you do this often?" Her chest clutched tight at the idea of Tope and Bosco with other women.

"Not often. There have been other women who were casual one night stands. Finding what we have

167

right now is difficult, near impossible. But there was someone, a while ago. We both wanted her. She wanted us. But she thought she could play us. She would be with me and then go to Bosco at a different time. She thought we didn't know what she was doing. So we decided to end the game. When she came here, Bosco was here. We offered her the same thing we're offering you now. But she ran. She couldn't handle that we both knew about each other and wanted her together."

He shook his head in a slow motion.

She saw the pain in his gaze. And Bosco's. The bitch had hurt them. "Tell me who the bitch is and where to find her so I can go and poke pins into her eyeballs for hurting you guys."

Bosco's chuckled and a smile bloomed on Tope's face. "Does that mean you accept us? No messing about, no running?"

"You are giving me something I've dreamt about." She met Bosco's smiling gaze. "The best deal I've ever had. I'm not stupid enough to screw it up or run from it."

"Good." Tope lowered his head and brushed his firm lips against hers. "Go and show Bosco how much you want him."

He lifted his head and leaned back into the sofa. She nodded and lowered her feet to the cool floor. Her legs wobbled. Tope's hand on her hip steadied her.

The space between where she stood and where Bosco sat was no more than three or four feet wide. But with butterflies in her belly, it felt as if a chasm separated them.

The first time she'd gone to Bosco, she'd been fuelled by anger added to lust. She hadn't cared for either man. Now, so much lay at stake than just physical desire. The men knew her too much. She couldn't walk away. No matter what happened, she would have to stay and work it out with them.

In this moment, it scared the shit out of her. There would be no place to run or hide.

Except into these men's arms. They would kill for her. Die for her. Die with her.

What more could she ask?

"Come here." Bosco stretched his hand out, as if sensing her turmoil. She looked into his eyes. They were amber brown, a little darker than whisky. Peace settled over her like a blanket. Bosco always had that effect on her.

Tope was intense, like an anchor keeping her secure and stable. Bosco made her feel as if she could fly above any turbulence.

She took a step, then another, put her left hand in his right. He tugged her onto his lap, his left palm cupping her cheek. His hand was cool, callused but somehow softer than Tope's. Also, he had long fingers and her pussy pulsed when she imagined him sliding them into her channel.

"I've wanted to kiss you for so long," he said before slanting his mouth across hers.

She gasped. She wasn't expecting his lips to be so supple. Unlike Tope with his fierceness, Bosco went slow, caressing, teasing before delving into her. He was sugar to Tope's spice, his taste sensual, evocative and intoxicating.

She moaned, grabbed his T-shirt, melting into him as heat coursed her veins. She came alive, floating into a heady space.

He broke the kiss and nibbled her lips, his fingers gently massaging her hip, just where the bone met flesh.

She moaned. She wanted him to keep kissing her.

Fingers swept hair over her right shoulder, and then lips were pressed against the skin on her nape. Tope was behind her, sitting on the sofa. His left hand stroked gently up and down her spine, right palm covering her right breast.

It was good but she needed more contact. "I...I need skin to skin. Please."

"It's okay. We'll take care of you," Bosco said in a low voice that made the butterflies flutter in her belly. He had a beautiful raspy tone to his voice.

A zipping sound cut through the sound of breathing. Bosco tugged the bottom hem of the dress.

"Raise you arms," Tope's deep voice whispered close to her left ear.

She did as instructed and Bosco pulled the outfit over her head and tossed it onto the other sofa.

Bosco sighed as his palms ghosted down her arms. "I'd almost forgotten how beautiful you are."

Warmth spread across her chest as she felt Tope unhook her bra and push the straps off her shoulders. Her boobs bounced as they were released. She wasn't small in that department. She had curves in abundance top and bottom. Bosco pulled the item and tossed it to join her dress, leaving her bare to their scorching gazes. Her already heated skin blazed and tingled.

Tope scooped her back onto his lap as he leaned on the arm of the three-seater. Her heart raced. Bosco hooked his fingers into her knickers and pulled them off. He got off the sofa and knelt between her splayed legs.

She was lying down, back to Tope's chest, her bum nestled on his crotch, right leg on top of his right on the sofa, left foot on the floor. Tope's palms kneaded the flesh of her tits. Bosco's hands were on her thighs. They were both still fully clothed.

"Guys, you're both still dressed." She squirmed as Tope pinched her nipples.

Bosco grinned. "We need to get you ready for us, babe. And I need to taste you."

Then his fingers parted her shaved lower lips and his tongue swiped upward from her slit.

"Ohhhh." She released a long moan, bowing off Tope's chest.

His hands squeezed her boobs, arms caging her. She was surrounded. Touched everywhere. Just the way she wanted it.

Bosco teased, prodded, twirled and poked with his tongue, his teeth grazing her labia and clit. Long fingers breached her entrance, filling her wet channel.

"That's it," Tope's husky voice whispered in her ear. "Relax, give yourself to us. You're in safe hands."

The combination of Tope's words and their actions sent her hurtling towards her first climax.

"Yes!" she cried out just as a finger entered her back hole. She panted as stars formed in the extremes of her vision.

The finger slid out and went in again as Bosco sucked hard on her clit. It distracted her when another finger joined the first one, filling her up.

She bowed, writhed as Tope pinched her nipples, sending an arc of pleasure straight to her clit.

"Oh...oh...oh," she sang in rhythm to Bosco's fingers pumping into her.

Tope leaned forward, turned her head and kissed her.

Then she was coming apart, eyes closed, thrashing about even as Tope held her together.

Bosco didn't stop until she went limp in Tope's arms. Tope broke the kiss and she panted for breath. She opened her eyes to find Bosco pulling his shirt off.

He really was a magnificent man. Where Tope was built with the sturdiness, Bosco had the lean grace. He was of ebony shade compared to Tope's chocolate skin tone. He was still a broad, tall man and as he chucked his jeans, his long, cut dick sprang free.

She licked her lips as he bent over, unlocked the drawer under the coffee table and pulled out a pack of condoms as well as a tube of lubricant.

"Bosco is going to fuck your pussy and I'm going to take your ass," Tope said and lifted her.

She stood on shaky legs and her body heated up. She'd had two men before but this was different. This would be the first time she had a man in both entrances at the same time.

Bosco rolled on a condom and lay back on the sofa, a sexy grin on his face. "Come on, babe. Time to ride my cock."

"Hell yeah," she said in a mock cowgirl tone as she sashayed over and climbed onto his lap. Settling with her knees on either side of his hips, she reached down and wrapped her hand around his length. She lowered onto the tip and pushed down.

Bosco gripped her hips as air whooshed out of him.

"Fuck, you feel good." He seemed to expand inside her. He lifted her and slammed her down. "Yes. So good."

He held her hips and jerked his. She clutched his chest and rode him in a slow rhythm.

"I could stand here watching the two of you. But I want to get inside her too," Tope said from over her shoulder.

She turned to find he was naked, standing behind her with a condom on as well. He held the tube of lube in his left hand as his right hand pressed between her shoulder blades.

"Lean over Bosco. Press your head to his chest if it's more comfortable."

She did as he said, gripping onto Bosco's shoulder, her head on his chest as she tried to look back. Bosco held her nape and leaned up to kiss her.

Cold gel drizzled down her crack and Tope's lubed cock pressed against her pucker. She stiffened, but someone's fingers—Bosco's, she guessed—stroked her clit, ramping up her pleasure as Tope pushed in.

"Damn, you're tight and hot and... so tight." Tope groaned.

She broke from the kiss, trying to draw in air into tight lungs. Her skin prickled with heat, sweat dripping down. Her heart raced. Her muscles relaxed as Tope slid out and Bosco slammed in. The men started alternating in filling her up, so that she felt full.

Pleasure speared through her. She felt lightheaded as if she was high on marijuana or some other drug. The men were fucking her at a steady rhythm. She had to get her breathing in tune so she didn't black out.

She whimpered, moaned, cried out. She felt so good. Tears welled up and dropped down her cheeks. Bosco leaned up, kissed her again as he slammed into her one last time and came.

A hand pressed down on her clit and black spots formed in her vision as a mind-blowing orgasm tore through her. She jerked so much, but the men held her together as she was caged between them. She must have blacked out for a few seconds because she wasn't aware of when Tope climaxed.

When she opened her eyes, Bosco was lifting her from the sofa and Tope wasn't in the living room.

"Where's...what's... going on?" Her brained refused to function and her words came out slurred.

"Don't worry, babe," Bosco said in a gentle voice. "We're just going to clean you up."

He carried her to the bathroom where Tope already had the warm water spraying from the shower unit. Bosco lowered her in the bath and used the soaped sponge to wash her before Tope rinsed her body off. He shut off the faucet and Bosco took the towel he held out to dry Anuli's body.

Then he lifted her out and across the hallway into the main bedroom. He laid her on the bed and pressed a kiss to her forehead before covering her with a sheet. There was a bottle of water and glass on the bedside cabinet.

He filled the glass with water and handed it to her. "Drink. Otherwise, you'll have a headache in the morning."

She sat up and gulped down the cool water. She hadn't realised she was so thirsty. She finished a second cupful before he returned the glass to the unit.

"You're not going to leave me here alone," she protested when he stood up.

"No. We're just going to clean up and then we'll join you in bed," he said.

"Okay." She curled up on her side and closed her eyes with a sigh. She was tired, in a good way, and she was looking forward to spending the night with both of them.

She drifted off to sleep and woke when she felt the bed depress and arms settled on her midriff as a hard body nestled behind her. Another pulled her so her cheek was on his chest.

She was covered by hard bodies that smelled of bergamot and spices. She had died and gone to Heaven. With a smile on her face, she drifted off to sleep again.

Chapter Seventeen

"Babe, wake up."

Someone shook her.

Anuli peeled groggy eyes open as she turned on her side. Dim light came in from the window. Someone sat on the bed beside her in jeans and no shirt, his back to her. He was bent forward as if pulling on shoes. A drop of water travelled down glistening skin too dark to be Tope's and yummy enough to lick.

It took a couple of seconds for her brain to process the person's identity. Bosco. He'd spent the night in the same bed as her and Tope. She'd woken up in the middle of the night hot and needing the bathroom only to find her body in a tangle of muscular limbs.

They'd woken as she'd climbed over Tope who lay closest to the door, Bosco reaching for her as Tope asked where she was going. She'd explained she'd needed to ease herself and they'd let her go.

The light hadn't come on when she'd flicked, another power cut, so she'd found her way to the bathroom in the dark. A sliver of moonlight had filtered in. Though, she was used to walking in the dark in this house so she knew her way around.

After doing her business, she'd washed with cold water from the tap and returned to the bedroom.

A little light came in through the curtained windows. But she saw the outline of the men sprawled on the bed, waiting for her, mocha and coffee. Tope had lifted her into bed, sliding her body over his until she settled back between the two men on her back.

"Are you sore?" Bosco's smoky voice whispered in her right ear as someone palmed her pussy.

"No," she replied, a little breathless as fingers stroked her. She trailed her hands down their rock abs until she found their jutting dicks.

"Good. Let's keep it that way." Tope's gravelly voice was in her left ear. "Go back to sleep. We have work tomorrow."

"Oh, come on. I'm a big girl. I can handle it." She kept stroking their cocks, one in each hand.

Bosco nuzzled her neck, his hand squeezing her right breast. At least she thought it was his hand from the angle. This meant it was probably Tope's palm teasing her wet pussy. She wanted one or both men inside her soon.

"Tiger, you're not going to miss work tomorrow. No matter what. Don't think you can sweet talk your way out of it."

"I won't dare," she teased. "Please, someone fuck me already."

Bosco chuckled. Tope landed a smack on her pussy.

"Aww." The sweet pain sent her body arching and her insides contracting.

"On your knees," Tope ordered.

That's how she ended up on all fours, sucking Tope's dick while Bosco fucked her from behind. She'd climaxed a couple of times before the men found their releases. They'd wiped down with a used T-shirt and slumped onto the sheets. It had felt so good at the time.

Now, she didn't want to get out of bed. Only wanted some more sleep. Her eyes drifted shut.

"Babe, you need to get out of bed before Tope gets in here. He's going to spank your ass if you don't."

Bosco's light warning made her open her eyes again.

"Where is he?" She sighed.

"In the kitchen, sorting out breakfast." He tugged on the other boot.

"You're not going to let him spank me, are you, Bosco?" She trailed her fingertips down her back. She'd already learned that he was the softie of the pair. He was more likely to give in to her request than Tope.

Chuckling, he turned around, the low light making his teeth glint. "Are you trying to bribe me?"

"Well, yes." She reached across and covered his groin with her hand. She could feel the heat of his stiffening shaft. "You can persuade him to let me stay home today and I'll give you the best blow job you ever had."

He groaned and brushed his left thumb across her lips. "Your mouth on my cock. So tempting."

"I promise it'll be worth it." She smiled up at him, hoping he'd be persuaded to let her have a day in bed.

She reached for his fly but he gripped her hand. "Not now."

He stood and picked up a T-shirt hanging over the armchair.

Footsteps announced Tope's arrival before she saw him. "Anuli, why are you still in bed?"

"She was trying to bribe me with a BJ so she wouldn't go to work today." Bosco flashed his teeth in a grin.

Shit. He'd just ratted her out. She frowned at him.

"Big mouth," she muttered under her breath.

"Naughty girl. Better get your big girl behind out of the bed before I batter it." Tope's threat held humour.

She shuffled her bum across the mattress and planted her feet on the floor.

"You are not my friend anymore." She pouted at Bosco who only chuckled.

Shaking her head, she padded across the room. "I wonder what the world is coming to when a girl can't offer an innocent BJ anymore to her men."

Tope's eyes twinkled with amusement. "Not when you're trying to get out of a promise you made. I warned you last night but you said you could handle it."

"I believe her words were 'can someone fuck me already'," Bosco mimicked her voice as he winked at her.

She couldn't help giggling and placed a hand on her left hip. "By the way, I don't sound like that."

Tope swatted her bum. "Move."

"Ouch," she yelped and ran into the bathroom, giggling.

"Be out in ten minutes," Tope ordered as she shut the door.

The smile stayed on her face as she brushed her teeth and showered. She'd never been so happy. Neither had she felt so possessed or protected. So taken care off.

Her body still buzzed from the sex although she wasn't excited about going to work today. She wasn't upset either. As long as she had Tope and Bosco around, she didn't care about anything else.

She came out to an empty bedroom and dressed quickly before heading out to the living room. Tope and Bosco were already at the dining table sharing a breakfast of akara, fried plantain slices and agidi.

"You didn't just make these," she asked as Tope pulled out a chair for her.

"No," he replied. "They are courtesy of Mama Ejima. I ordered last night and Nonso delivered the food this morning."

A fluttery feeling settled in her stomach. Tope kept surprising her. She'd admit she was no domestic goddess. Although Anuli could cook, Tessa had been the chef when they lived together.

Now living in a house with two men, people would be surprised that Tope spent more time in the kitchen or sorting out their meals than she did. Neither Bosco nor Tope seemed interested in turning her into their domestic servant, cooking and cleaning up after them. They handled their own messes.

She leaned across and pressed a kiss to Tope's cheek before piling food in her plate.

"Why does he get a kiss and I don't?" Bosco asked, brow raised although his lips tugged up at the corner.

"You ratted on me. You're not my friend anymore." She stuck her tongue out at him.

"Hey. He's the one who spanked your bum," Bosco protested with a laugh.

"And he's the one who ordered my favourite breakfast." She pouted before picking up an akara and taking a bite. She mewled at the taste of the fried beans ball.

Tope laughed and shook his head at both of them. Bosco winked at her.

After the meal, she piled the dishes in the sink. She would deal with them when they got back from work as they were already running later than their usual schedule. Getting stuck in Port Harcourt morning traffic was no fun.

When they got home that evening, Bosco wasn't there. She assumed he'd come over later but he didn't. It wasn't until they were getting ready for bed that she asked Tope who explained that Bosco had gone to sort out the safe house they would need when they captured Uncle Joe. Bosco would be back in a few days once he'd secured the premises.

Tope also told her that Siki was part of a two-man team running surveillance on Uncle Joe. They'd also travelled up to Makurdi today.

A fluttery, empty sensation sat with Anuli for the rest of the week as the thing she'd wanted for so long seemed to be within reach. She fantasised about what would happen once they finally got a hold of her stepfather. She feared that something would go wrong to screw things up. And she worried that Tope and Bosco would get arrested and locked up for what they were planning.

For the nights that Bosco was away, she didn't sleep properly as her worry increased. Tope reassured her that everything would be all right and that she should stop over-thinking things.

Since Bosco hadn't called, she worried that something bad had happened to him. Tope said the other man was probably in a location with little or no network coverage, so he wouldn't be able to contact them.

On Friday evening, they arrived home to find Bosco's bike parked under the car port.

"He's home," Anuli exclaimed and pushed open the car door. She rushed across the veranda, leaving Tope to lock up the gates.

"Bosco," she called out as soon as she opened the front door. "Bosco!"

She popped her head through the living room but he wasn't there and she checked the kitchen too. She collided with him as he came out of the bathroom fresh from the shower.

"Hey, Babe." He held her arms, steadying her when she would have tumbled backward.

"You're home," she squealed, wrapped her arms around his shoulders and hugged him tight.

"Someone missed me," he said in an amused tone. "I thought I wasn't your friend any longer."

She leaned back and swatted his shoulder. "Of course I missed you, fool. You didn't tell me you were going away and then you didn't call for days. Kiss me already."

With one hand on her bum and the other on her cheek, he lowered his head and kissed her.

"Mmmmhhmmm," she moaned as heat flared inside her. She anchored her arms around him and wrapped her legs around his hips.

His towel fell off as he grabbed her ass, holding her to him so that she felt his rigidity between her thighs. They moaned and ground against each other as he carried her into the bedroom. Then he broke the kiss and fumbled around in the bedside top drawer.

"I'm going to fuck you." He pulled out a condom and then braced her against the wall.

She heard the sound of the tearing foil and then he reached down to roll it on. A movement by the door made her glance in that direction. It was Tope leaning against the post, a grin on his face. He didn't move to join them, just folded his arms across his chest.

"Give our Bosco a very good welcome home." Tope winked at her. He was giving her and Bosco this moment but still being a part of it. She'd never met a man like him who didn't feel threatened that another man was getting attention from his woman. That another man was fucking her.

Since she'd met Tope, it was as if she was catching up on all those miserable birthdays and special moments she'd missed out on as a child. She could never let go of him, no matter what.

She smiled as Bosco's fingers shoved her panties aside, then moaned as his cock rammed into her. Then he was pounding into her against the wall. All the while, Tope stood there watching them, his gaze locked on to her.

Her body heated, her skin prickled as pleasure swarmed her from top to bottom. Her pussy clamped around Bosco's cock again and again. His grip on her ass tightened.

"I'm not going to last," Bosco panted the words. "Babe, reach between us and touch your clit for me."

She did as he instructed as fever spread through and her climax peaked. "Yes!"

"Damn," he cried out and jerked his hips as he came.

They both stilled, panting for breath, his sweaty forehead resting on hers.

"Welcome home," she said and bit the corner of her lower lip.

"Thank you, babe." His grin was beautiful and sexy.

"Right. Clean up, people. We're going to Mama Ejima's for some food," Tope said before he disappeared down the corridor.

Chapter Eighteen

Bosco killed the engine of the power bike in front of the pedestrian gate to Anuli's old accommodation.

Anuli placed her left foot on the ground and swung her right leg as she climbed down. Her legs wobbled a little as she caught her breath. Riding on Bosco's motorcycle made her feel exhilarated as well as aroused.

She pushed the helmet off her head and ran fingers through the hair to tame any unruly strands.

Bosco pulled his protective visor off too, still astride the motorbike. "Are you sure you're going to be okay?"

"Of course I'm going to be all right," she replied, beaming a smile at him. She loved that her men were so protective. This was her old neighbourhood and she could take care of herself.

"Okay. I won't be too long. Don't go anywhere," he said as he reached for the ignition.

"I won't." She bent forward and pressed a kiss to his lips.

His eyes twinkled as he replaced his helmet over his head and kick started the engine. The floor beneath her sandals vibrated. Then he was gone.

She turned around to find the gateman stood watching with the gate open. She hadn't even knocked yet. The man was a busybody.

"Aunty, you don come? E don tey since we see you," the man said in way of greeting as he backed up for her to enter the compound.

"Oga gateman, how now?" She asked how he was to be pleasant.

"You don see us now. Na how you leave us, na so we dey." The man flashed a set of crooked teeth.

"Madam Landlady, she dey for house?" she asked.

"Eh, she never comot. So she dey inside." He pointed at the big detached two-level house that was the landlord's family home.

She walked to the front door and rang the bell. The door was opened by the woman she wanted to see. Anuli greeted her and explained the reason she was there. She'd decided not to renew her tenancy and would be moving out. The woman said she was sorry to be losing Anuli but she'd suspected that might be the case since Tessa moved out. She wished Anuli the best of luck for the future.

Anuli thanked her and walked down the side of the building to the two level Boy's Quarters that housed her rented room. She'd decided to move out since Tessa wasn't coming back. Tope's house was now her home anyway.

Tope had travelled on Monday for the official opening of Park Hotel Calabar on Tuesday. He was scheduled to return to Port Harcourt today and would come here so she could load his car with the items she was taking with her.

In Tope's absence, Bosco had stepped up. He had taken her to work on his bike and picked her up at the end of her shifts for the first two days of the week. But she'd now caught up on the hours she'd missed from her previous absences and with a new school year only a couple of weeks away, she would return to working just weekends.

Anuli glanced at her watch. It was just before noon. She was thirsty and could use something to eat. She glanced at the items scattered all over the bed. She would take a break and come back to finish the packing when she'd eaten something. There was a shop at the top of the street where she could buy a snack and drinks.

She left her room, locked the door and headed out. She was walking down the street when her phone rang.

***

Bosco checked the stash of weapons he'd just picked up—two AK-47 assault rifles, One Smith & Wesson Shield 9 and a Colt 45 semi hand guns—and ammunitions. He double-checked the cartridge boxes, making sure they had enough for what they needed. It was his job to deal with the logistics.

He'd sorted out the safe house, a location close to Benue River between Makurdi and Gboko, near Abinsi. It helped that he understood some Tiv and spoke Idoma well. As a young boy, he'd found he had a knack for languages and these days his work meant that he travelled to different places. It also helped that he'd been up there before.

Tomorrow, they would travel up to Makurdi and finally put their plans into action. He couldn't wait to get his hands on Anuli's stepfather and his cohorts and dish out some jungle justice.

Anuli thought he was just a weapons dealer. But in truth, he was more than that. He was a chameleon. The things he'd done in the name of his country and the law were numerous. Yet he would never receive a commendation for those things.

He had given a lot, sacrificed even more. The scars on his body stood as proof.

This time, though, it was personal. Anuli was a great woman and he cared about her. Finding out what had happened to her only filled him with cold rage. Nothing was going to save her stepfather from his wrath. Unless the man died before Bosco got his hands on him.

According to the reports from Siki, the man was alive and going about his normal routine.

Bosco locked the weapons back in the case and put it into the hidden space at the bottom of the wardrobe before replacing the false bottom and piling the shoes back on top. To anyone else, it looked like any normal wardrobe and it would have to take a diligent person and tearing the unit aside to find the secret stash.

He would be back tomorrow to pick up the items and put them in Tope's car on their way north.

He grabbed the helmet he'd left on the table and stepped to the door. Then he activated the battery-powered motion sensor which would send an alert to his phone if anyone walked into his room before shutting and locking the door.

People in the area knew him by reputation if not personally and they feared him. So no one dared to break into his space. But he couldn't be complacent. There was always the exception to every rule. He was a maverick and he dared to go where no one else went. This meant there would always be people like him who would step into the lion's den just for the hell of it.

The sun was high in the sky as he got on this bike. The girl in the shop next door waved at him as he wore his helmet. He waved back and he started the engine. Then he turned the bike around and rode down the gently sloping sandy street back towards the main road leading to where Anuli lived.

Post-lunchtime traffic meant there were a lot of cars on the road. It didn't affect him as he navigated his bike through the bottlenecks and arrived in front of the gates he'd dropped Anuli off thirty minutes after he left his house.

***

Tope finished the meeting with the Deputy Head of Security for Park Hotel, Port Harcourt. He'd arrived back from Calabar this morning. The opening ceremony for the new hotel had gone without a hitch. Peter Oranye, Paul Arinze and Michael Ede, the three owners, had been there for the launch. Tope had formally handed over to the Calabar Head of Security before driving down to PHC.

Now he'd just been briefed on the past few days and was also making sure that everything he needed to deal with was done as he was taking a week off work. The people at Park Hotel's didn't know why. They thought he was travelling to visit family.

He needed the time off for the mission they'd planned. Everything was now in place. Surveillance. Weapons. Safe house. Take down sequence. All that needed to be done was for them to go up to Benue State and pick up the target.

He, Bosco and Anuli would be doing that tomorrow.

A knock sounded at the door to his office on the ground floor of the hotel.

"Come in," he said as he looked up.

The door pushed inward and Joy walked in. She wasn't dressed in the housekeeping uniform which meant she'd completed her shift or wasn't working today.

"Joy, how can I help you?" He hadn't spoke to the girl in weeks and wondered what she was doing here.

Smiling coquettishly, she shut the door and walked across the room. She leaned her hip at the edge of his desk in a familiar gesture. "I wanted to talk to you about something."

"Sit in the chair and talk," he said in a cold voice, not wanting to encourage her. He couldn't forget that she'd been gossiping about Anuli.

She flustered, a frown on her face before she slid into the padded seat. Her throat bobbed as she swallowed. She leaned forward, arm on thighs, which pushed her chest forward, showing off her boobs in the low-cut neck line.

"Your girlfriend is no good for you," she said in a low conspiratorial tone. "You go away for a few days and she's all over town with other men."

Tope leaned back in his chair and raised his eyebrow. "What are you talking about?"

"Yesterday and the day before, she came to work riding on the back of a man's bike," Joy said in disgust.

Tope pretended he didn't know what she was talking about. "That is probably an okada man dropping her because I wasn't here to bring her to work."

"Okada man ke. You should see the way she was kissing and hugging him shamelessly as if people cannot see them. That was no okada man o. The same man dropped and picked her two days in a row."

Tope shook his head slowly. He didn't need people to tell him what Anuli was up to.

"See, that girl is no good for you," Joy continued as she got off the chair and came around the table. "After everything you do for her, she cheats on you like that. I will never do that to you."

He gripped her arm when she tried to touch his chest. "I've told you before I'm not interested in making you my girlfriend. We fucked once and that was a mistake. It won't happen again."

She gasped, mouth dropping open.

"I love Anuli and nothing you say about her is going to change that. So get out of my office before I make you wish you never met me."

He let go of her arm and she staggered back.

She kept glancing at him, shock on her face and head bowed as she hurried to leave his office.

He puffed out a breath after she left and lowered his body back into the padded office chair. He needed to get out of here soon. His phone beeped and he pulled it out of his pocket.

"Bosco," he said into the mouth piece.

"Tope, we have a problem," his friend replied in a shaky voice.

His heart jolted and he sat straight. Bosco was supposed to be with Anuli. "What happened?"

"I can't find Anuli. She's missing."

Chapter Nineteen

Tope's heart froze. Anuli was missing? No, it couldn't be. He sat rigidly with his hand gripping the phone tight.

"Explain." There was a tremor in his voice as he spoke.

Rustling and crackling on the line indicated that Bosco was moving, probably pacing. The revving of an engine announced he stood on the street. Outside Anuli's house?

"I dropped her off at her old place this morning so she could start packing her things. The plan was that I would come back and help her finish off while we waited for you to bring the car to load up. I left her around ten o'clock, went to pick up the things we discussed and came back about thirty minutes ago."

Tope glanced at his watch. Two forty-eight PM.

"I called her phone but there was no response, thought she was probably away from it and knocked at the gates. The gate man said she walked out about an hour earlier and hadn't returned. I tried her phone again and still no answer. So I convinced the gate man to let me in and went inside to check her room. The door is locked but I can see inside from the windows. She's not in there. I came out and walked down the street and asked the shopkeepers. No one has seen her. So I called you. Did she mention she was going somewhere else?"

"No." Tope rubbed his hand on the back of his head. "The only thing we discussed was about her moving out of the place. She knew I was back in Port Harcourt today."

He pushed off the chair abruptly, making it bang against the back wall.

"You don't think she's gone to see a friend?" Bosco asked as if he sensed his friend's rising tension.

"Then she should've called you or me to say where she'd gone," Tope snapped. A sheen of sweat broke on his skin and he felt the beginning of a headache. If Anuli had gone off somewhere without informing anyone, he was so going to make her bum sore when he got his hands on her.

"Yes, she would have. She wouldn't be that unthinking," Bosco said in an even voice to calm him. "I'm going to look around again. Maybe she just went to get something to eat and forgot the time."

Tope sucked in a deep breath. Anuli could be rash sometimes. He'd seen her do some crazy things, so this wasn't beyond her capabilities. But she'd mellowed a little since she'd been spending time with him and Bosco and she would know that there would be a consequence to her actions.

"Okay. Let me know as soon as you find her. I'm going to wrap up here and come to you," Tope replied.

"No wahala." Bosco hung up.

Tope placed his phone on the table and gripped the edge of the table, sucking and expelling air slowly. Although he wanted to think that Bosco was right and Anuli had just wandered off, he couldn't shake the niggling in the back of his mind that something else was responsible for her absence.

What if she'd finally found a way to leave him? She'd been threatening to do so from the first day he'd brought her to his house.

His chest constricted, making it hard to breathe. His throat tightened in pain and he swallowed hard.

Losing her would devastate him. Knowing what he knew about her, he'd loved her more, not less. She was a fighter. His tiger.

He'd sworn to kill for her and he'd surely die to protect her. She knew this already. Wasn't it enough for her? What else could he do to prove himself?

Buzz. Buzz. His vibrating phone moved around the wooden table top.

He snatched it, pressed the green answer button as he lifted it to his ear. "Yes."

"You need to come down here. Someone saw a woman arguing with a man as she got dragged into a vehicle," Bosco said.

"I'm on my way." Tope snatched his keys and headed for the door.

***

Anuli pulled her phone out of her bag. She recognised the number. Regina. She hadn't spoken to the girl since they saw each other weeks ago.

Regina had called her a few times but Anuli hadn't answered the call.

This time, she pressed the green button. "Regina, how now?"

"Anuli, hi. I finally got a hold of you." The girl sounded relieved and annoyed at the same time.

Anuli grimaced. She stopped at the corner of the street and leaned against the security wall. The shop she needed was just around the bend. It was a hot afternoon and this space had a large tree which provided some shade from the hot sun. "Sorry. I told you I was going to be busy."

"I know. I came to your place a few times and they said they hadn't seen you for a while." Regina sighed. "So how was your trip?"

"It was good," she lied. She couldn't say that she had postponed the trip or that she was moving out of the place.

A dark blue SUV pulled up in front of her. A man sat at the driver's seat. There was a woman in the front passenger seat. She saw the hair extensions but not the face. But the back windows were blacked out so she couldn't see who was in there. Her spine stiffened and she straightened. The car seemed familiar but she couldn't place it.

"Great. Can I come and see you?" Regina said in her ear, distracting her from what was going on in front of her.

"No. It's not a good idea." She kept her gaze on the car. Something about the way the man looked at her made her skin prickle. "Look, Regina. I can't see you anymore. There's someone else."

The woman in the car lifted her hand, pointing in Anuli's direction as her face came into view.

Anuli gasped. "Joy?"

What was the woman doing here, pointing at her?

"You're seeing someone else?" Regina asked in an upset voice on the phone.

But Anuli didn't register the girl's pain as her attention was now fully on the car. The back door open and a man stepped out. He was dressed in sky blue shirt, dark jeans and black boots. He looked official in a casual way.

"Anuli Okoro?" the man asked as he stepped over the gutter at the edge of the pavement.

She glanced up and down the street. This area was quiet as the place she'd lived in was a cul-de-sac, which meant there was no through traffic. The busy street was just round the corner. Cars drove by but none turned in her direction.

"Yes." She tilted her chin up. She wouldn't be cowered, even if Joy had hired thugs to intimidate her. "What is this about?"

"You need to come with us." The man had reached her now.

The muscles on his dark skin stretched the fabric of his shirt. He had a sneer on his face.

"Who are you and what do you want?" she snapped at him. She wasn't going anywhere with them.

"You'll find out when we get to our destination. There's someone who wants to see you."

"Someone who wants to see me? You mean that bitch, Joy. I'm happy to see her any time." She stepped to the car, bypassing the man. "You want to see me, Joy? Why don't you come out and we'll settle this right here and right now."

Joy just turned her face away.

Anuli shook her head. "Coward. You had to hire thugs to fight for you. Well, I can handle them."

The man beside her grabbed her arm and tugged.

"Leave me alone," she shouted.

The man hit her between the shoulders and she toppled forward. She lifted her hands to break her fall and hit the back seat of the car. The man lifted her legs with both hands and shoved her in.

Anuli kicked and fought, banging her head and arms against the door and head rest. The man struck her across the face with one hand and shut the door with the other. The car sped off in a squeal of tyres and dust.

"Fuck you. Let me go." She scratched and snarled at the man beside her.

The man was strong and her attempts to fight him off didn't work. He yanked her hair and covered her mouth with a damp cloth. She struggled to breathe before blacking out.

***

Tope was with Bosco within thirty minutes. The other man had commandeered the outside sitting area of a restaurant.

Bosco introduced the dark-skinned girl in a blue check dress and a black apron. "This is Ngozi. She's the one who saw the incident in the car."

"Tell me what happened," Tope said as he sat down opposite the girl.

"I dey wash plate for back. Na when I hear person dey shout. I look up, see this woman dey fight with one man like that for road. The man carry am enter car. The car drive comot."

"Did you see the woman? Is this her?" Tope pulled his phone out and swiped to a photo of Anuli taken in his house only a few days ago. She'd been in the kitchen smiling up at him, her hand on her hip in a teasing pose.

"Eh, na she be that. I know this aunty. She dey come here from time to time. Although I never see am for long time."

She'd just confirmed it had been Anuli arguing with a man before being dragged into a car.

Tope's heart raced but he maintained outward calm so he could get as much information from the girl. "Did you see the man? Can you describe him?"

The girl frowned. "The man dark like this uncle." She indicated Bosco with the tilt of her head. "But he no tall like am. And him hair dey short like your own. I no see him face well well. But he wear shirt like your own. I think na blue. Him trouser na black."

Bosco was typing on his phone taking a note of what the girl said.

"Good. What about the car? What kind was it?" Tope asked.

She squeezed her face again. "E be like your own. The colour maybe na black maybe na navy. I no remember. But na big car. I remember say mud dey for the side and me I dey wonder why the driver no wash car for oga this morning."

That was crucial information. It hadn't rained locally for a few days and the ground was dry. Mud instead of dust implied the car had waded through wet earth recently. Also, she was right. Someone who drove a car like that should be conscious about keeping it clean. So it was peculiar that it hadn't been washed in a few days.

"What else do you remember? Was it just one man in the car? Was there anyone else close by?"

She shifted from one foot to the other. "I see driver for front and I think say woman dey front as well but I no sure."

That made at least two other people in the car. He glanced at Bosco who met his gaze and gave him a slight tip of head. Bosco was indicating that the girl was holding out on something which Tope agreed on too.

He focused his attention back on her. He swiped the screen of his phone again so that Anuli's picture reappeared.

"Ngozi," he said in a low calm voice. "Anuli is my wife and I'm worried she may have been kidnapped. You understand that I would like to do everything I can to find her. I'm going to give a reward to anyone who can help me get her back."

He pulled out his wallet from his back pocket so she could see he was serious. "Is there anything else you can tell me that will help me find her?"

The girl shifted again, glanced around the room before sighing. "Make you follow me."

Tope glanced at Bosco before walking behind the girl down a side passage. She walked to the large blue plastic water reservoir that sat on a concrete elevation. She shoved her hand into the space between the tank and the grey concrete wall and pulled out a black plastic bag.

She held the bag out in this direction. "Abeg, no vex. I see the phone for ground when the car comot. It just dey there. I think say I go give aunty when I see am again."

Tope's heart raced as he tore the bag open and pulled out a phone. Anuli's phone. He unlocked the screen and saw all the missed calls from him and Bosco.

Now at least he knew why Anuli wasn't answering her phone. She wasn't with it.

Shit. She really was in trouble if she'd dropped her phone in the struggle with whoever had taken her. Shit. His hand shook as adrenaline coursed through him.

"Abeg. Sorry," the girl in front of him pleaded.

He wasn't sure if the girl really meant to give the phone back to Anuli or whether she'd planned to keep it to herself. At least the girl had given it to him. He was grateful for that.

"It's okay. Thank you for giving me the phone." He pulled some notes out of his wallet and reached out to Ngozi.

She shook her head. "Uncle, no need. I just want make you find Aunty Anuli."

He nodded, swivelled and went back into the restaurant.

"Anuli's phone." He showed Bosco the gadget. "The girl picked it up from the pavement after the car drove away."

"Damn." Bosco gripped the back of a plastic chair. "We have to find her."

"I know," he gritted out. Where to start? They could have tracked the signal from her phone but that was now out of the question.

He walked out into the bright sunshine, squinting as he looked up and down the street. Bosco followed him. He strode down and to the side street that Anuli lived on. He stopped at the spot on the pavement under the tree.

He tried to work out what had happened.

"So we know she left her house and walked down the pavement. But she never reached the main street because she got dragged into a car at about this point.

Bosco walked on to the unpaved road, bent over and held his camera out and took photos.

"What is it?" Tope asked.

"Tyre tracks." Bosco pointed at the jagged imprint on the dry ground. "It matches what the girl said. A car stopped at this spot and the spray of dirt showed it drove off at speed."

Tope nodded. "So she walked up to this point and a car stopped in front of her. But she lives in a cul-de-sac so where did the car come from? Were they parked up waiting for her or did they just arrive as she came out?"

"There's an arched trail which indicates that they may have arrived, seen her and turned around."

"I think so too." Tope looked at Anuli's phone that was still in his hand. He couldn't bring himself to put it away. It was his only link to her at the moment. "She must have had her phone in her hand when she dropped it which could mean she was talking to someone on the phone."

He unlocked the screen again and scrolled through the calls. Before all the missed calls from him and Bosco, there were two calls from someone named Regina. Anuli had told him about a girl he'd dated called Regina.

He pressed the button and dialled the number. It rang a couple of times before it was answered.

"Anuli?" a girl asked in a tentative voice.

"Is this Regina?" he asked in a mellow voice.

"Yes. Who are you?"

"My name is Tope. I don't know if Anuli told you about me."

"Which Tope?"

He tried not to grit his teeth. "Tope from Park Hotel. I saw you and her the other time at DJ Bar."

"Oh, yes. I remember," she said and paused. "Are you with Anuli? Is she okay?"

He evaded the question as he didn't want to divulge anything yet. "I'm hoping you can help me. You spoke to Anuli this afternoon, right?"

"Yes. I called her and was chatting with her. Then she seemed to ignore me. I could hear her talking to someone else in the background. They were arguing before the line went dead. I called her back but she didn't answer. Is she okay?"

"That's what I want to find out. Can you remember what she was arguing about with the man?"

"I don't know exactly. She sounded angry." Regina paused. "She mentioned the name Joy. There was a woman there also."

Tope's spine prickled. "Joy? Are you sure that's the name you heard?"

"Yes, of course I'm sure. She told me she'd met someone else. The next thing she was calling out Joy. I can never forget that name."

"Okay. Was there anything else?"

"No. Anyway, what is this about? Where is Anuli? Can I talk to her?"

"Thank you for your help, Regina. I'll let Anuli know you were asking about her." He cut off the phone line.

"Who is Joy?" Bosco asked as soon as he lowered the phone. The man must have detected an inflection in Tope's voice when he'd said the name.

"Joy is a girl at work that I had a thing with a long time ago. She had an altercation with Anuli and this afternoon she came into my office trying to get back together with me." Tope headed back towards his car.

"You think she arranged this?" Bosco asked, matching his steps.

"I don't know but it's not beyond her. And it's the only lead we have at the moment." Tope glanced at her watch. "She won't be at work but I know where she lives."

"I'm coming with you," Bosco said as they reached his bike first.

Tope nodded. He didn't expect anything less from his friend. "Just follow me."

Bosco swung his leg over the machine and pulled his helmet on.

Tope pressed the key fob as he reached the car. He pulled the door open and got into the driver's seat. His hand shook as he put the key into the ignition. He gripped the steering wheel, sucked in a deep breath before he put the car in gear, glanced in his mirror, flicked the indicator and pulled into the traffic.

Chapter Twenty

Jolting motion woke Anuli. Disorientated, she peeled her eyes open and looked around. Her head ached as her eyes adjusted to the darkness. She lay across the back seat of a car. Low light from the dials on the dashboard illuminated the interior. There were two men sitting up front. She recognised them from this afternoon. The men who had taken her. Where was Joy? And where were they driving to?

From this angle, she couldn't see much out of the blacked out windows. But they had to be on a road in the middle of nowhere as there were no street lights. An occasional beam from a passing car lit the interior.

She tried to sit up but bit back a moan instead. Her hands hurt where they were tied together with rope and her body felt bruised from where she had been rough-handled when she'd fought him. A tape sealed her mouth so she couldn't speak.

Who the hell were these people and what did they want from her?

She growled and bucked, swinging her legs off the edge of the seat. The car went over a pothole that sent her crashing into the back of the seat. She groaned.

The man in the passenger chair turned around and looked at her. In the shadow, his menacing grin appeared demonic. "Stay down," he barked out.

Her heart raced, exploding in her chest. Her body heaved up and down as she breathed heavily.

What had Joy told them to do to her? This was Nigeria. The possibilities were endless. Were they going to kill her and dump her in the middle of nowhere? A little extreme but still...

There were always stories of people being used for money rituals.

This sent her into a mix of panic and anger. She just couldn't lie here and wait for whatever they were going to dish out.

Her hands were tied to her legs so she couldn't even lift it to her face. She swung her legs again. This time, the bump in the road sent her in the right direction. She fell forward into the space between the front and back seats on her hands and knees.

Her body hurtled, her side hitting the back of the front seat as the car screeched to a halt. The man in the passenger seat shoved his door open.

Anuli scrambled to push off the floor before he could reach her. The door to the back yanked open and he loomed before her. As she was still on her knees on the floor, she couldn't see past him at this angle.

"I told you to stay still." He grabbed her arm in a tight grip, hurting her. He yanked her back onto the seat.

"Ouch," she protested but the sound was muffled by the gag. The pain made her eyes water. She blinked it back. She wouldn't let him see her in pain. He would enjoy it too much. She muttered behind the gag, indicating with her head that she wanted to go out.

The guy in the driver's seat had turned around to watch them now that the interior light illuminated the space. He looked a little more detached from the situation than his friend.

She muttered again, appealing to him with her eyes.

He glanced at his companion. "Let's find out what she wants."

"I don't have to listen to anything she has to say," the man outside said.

Her eyes went wide and she turned to the driver, mumbling some more.

The driver reached across and tugged the corner of the tape over her lips and yanked.

"Ouch!" she cried out, her mouth now open.

"What is it?" the man standing outside barked.

Anuli swallowed and moved her jaw. It ached a bit but her tongue worked. "I want to wee unless you want me to do it in the car."

"Fuck that. You're not messing up this car." The driver scrambled out of the car. He came around as the other man moved out of the way. "Out!"

"I can't walk in these." She indicated the rope wound around her arms and legs.

He walked back to the front, reached across and opened the glove compartment where he pulled out a big knife with a jagged edge.

Her breath hitched and she watched him closely as he came back. "I'm going to let you loose so you can do your business. Don't think of running away. There's nobody here to help you and we left the nearest town two hours back which means it would take you longer to walk. When you finish, you're going to come back and sit quietly until we reach where we're going."

She nodded at him.

"Otherwise, we will tie you back up, stuff you in a bag and put you in the boot."

The thought of not being able to talk or see or move made her shudder. "I won't be any trouble."

"Good." He sliced the bonds off. "Out."

She rubbed her wrists as she shuffled out of the car and gingerly placed her feet on the ground. The area was dark, the only light from the headlights. Trees and shrubs loomed ahead like silent ghouls and she shuddered again.

She stepped further and stumbled at the uneven ground. Grass and leaves scratched her skin and the temperature had dropped so she shivered some more.

The first man matched her steps about two feet to her right. He held a small black gun in his right hand.

"Are you going to watch me?" she asked, wondering if she could create enough space between them so she could run away.

He didn't say anything, just kept his gaze on her. She groped in the dark until she reached a spot where she thought he couldn't see her. She squatted but she didn't take her jeans off. She crept forward in the grass, keeping low. She stopped, listened to see if he was following. He wasn't. She crawled a bit further. Twigs and stone dug into her palms. She hoped she didn't step on a snake or scorpion or some other creepy crawly. She crept forward again.

Suddenly, hands grabbed her head and yanked her backward. She screamed, hands gripping the person's muscular arms. He lifted her as if she weighed nothing and crashed through the shrubs as he headed back towards the car.

She shouted and fought as the second man opened the boot of the car and the other one tossed her into it. She landed with a thud and banged her head against something metallic. She cried out.

"I warned you," one of them snarled as he covered her face with the chloroform cloth and she blacked out again.

Chapter Twenty One

The sun was low in the sky when Tope arrived at Joy's house. He remembered where she lived because he'd dropped her home once. Otherwise, he would've had to extract her address from her employee file at Park Hotel.

Joy's apparent involvement in Anuli's abduction meant she had flouted several of the employment terms and conditions. At the least, she faced termination of employment and at the most, arrest, prosecution and a long jail term.

Tope drove the car into the dusty front yard of a single level house. He got out and shut the door. A thunking sound drew his attention to three teenage boys sitting on a low grey brick fence to the right. One of them threw a faded blue ball at the wall. *Thunk.* It bounced back and he caught it, repeating the motion.

He stopped bouncing the ball and spoke. "Uncle, who you dey find?"

"I came to see Joy. Can you go and call her for me?" Tope withdrew a note from his wallet to encourage the boy to move.

The lad smiled and jumped off the wall. "I go call am for you."

He strode up the short concrete steps leading to the terrace and down the shadowed corridor which split the house in two.

Tope heard Bosco's bike rather than saw his friend pull up and kill the engine. He didn't look in Bosco's direction. They'd already agreed that Bosco would keep out of view. They didn't want to spook Joy.

"She dey come," the boy said when he came out.

Tope extended his hand with money and the boy took it, rejoining his friends who started chatting about what to do with the money.

A minute later, Joy appeared at the entrance. She froze when she saw Tope, a frown on her face. "Tope, what are you doing here?"

Tope forced a smile on his face and shook out his tight shoulders. "Hi, Joy. I came to see you."

She averted her gaze and bit her lip. "I thought you said..."

He took steps towards her. "Don't mind what I said in the office. I was just a bit tired. I found out that what you said about Anuli was true and I came to take you out to my house."

Tope was encouraging her delusion but it was the only way he knew to snare her to come with him willingly so he could extract information from her. He didn't want to get the police involved at this moment, as they would only delay the search for Anuli.

Joy's lips parted and her expression softened. "Really?"

"Yes. Why else would I come here? Can we go to my place?" He forced the smile to remain on his face.

"Yes, of course. Let me get changed."

"No. There's no need for that." He didn't have time for more delays. "You look lovely as you are. Come on."

Her smile widened and she batted her long fake lashes. "Okay. Let me get my bag."

"Be quick."

She disappeared indoors.

Tope glance at his watch. It was about two hours since Bosco had first called him about Anuli's disappearance. If Joy was in her house, then what did the men who took Anuli do with her?

Boulders lodged in his gut and his heart raced at the possibilities. He just wouldn't consider the worst-case. Anuli was still alive and he would find her.

Joy came out again. She'd swapped her rubber flip-flops for leather sandals and carried a small black bag.

He avoided her gaze as he opened the passenger door for her. His grip tightened on the handle. This was a gesture he reserved for Anuli but only carried it out now for the sake of the charade.

When she sat down, he shut the door and hurried to the other side. A few seconds later, he was back on the road.

"We're going to do a quick stopover before going to my house," he said before glancing in Joy's direction.

"Okay," she replied, looking too comfortable in the car.

He maintained his gaze on the road as his temple throbbed. In his line of work, he'd seen all sorts of people and all sorts of criminals. He understood that sometimes, people had to do wrong things in order to survive certain situations.

But when someone actually went out to hurt other people for their own gain, any empathy he had vanished. This was one of the main reasons he did his job—protecting others.

Although he'd had one night of sex with Joy and the woman had wanted more from him, he hadn't been able to touch her again. Not after he'd witnessed the way she behaved towards other staff.

And her altercation with Anuli only proved that Joy was a bully. And now he knew she was a woman who would harm others to get whatever she wanted.

Instead of heading to his house—he wouldn't soil the space with Joy's presence. Not to mention that Anuli would kill him for taking another woman there—he headed for the secure premises they used to detain individuals who'd committed an offence at Park Hotel before they were transferred to police custody.

Half an hour later, the gateman let him into security premises. He parked at his spot and killed the engine.

"Should I wait in the car?" Joy asked.

Tope ignored her. He no longer had to play nice. He got out of the car, walked around and yanked her door open. "Get out."

Her head jerked back, eyes widened. "What?"

He reached across, unclipped her seatbelt and grabbed her arm.

"What's going on?" she asked in a stunned voice as he pulled her from the car.

"You'll find out shortly." He held onto her arm, making her stagger her steps as he dragged her into the building.

At the desk, he logged her in for the record. "John, this is Joy Etuk. She is here for questioning on a kidnapping."

John scribbled on the notebook on the desk. Joy stiffened beside him and a gasp escaped her. He ignored her and continued. "Once I finish with her, we need to arrange to hand her over to the local police. Call our liaison at CID and report it. They need to send officers to pick her up."

"Okay, sir. Interview room one is free." John picked up a key from a hook behind the counter and passed it to Tope.

"I don't know what this is about. You have to let me go." Joy tried to pry his fingers off with the other hand.

He just ignored her and dragged her into the interview room. The room was bare except for a table with a bench on one side and another on the other side.

"Sit down," he ordered as he pointed at the bench.

She flinched and lowered her body on the seat. Sweat coated her face and she kept blinking. He stepped out and slammed the door shut. He would give her a few minutes to stew while he waited for Bosco to arrive.

There was a camera in the room and the video feed was displayed on the monitor behind the front desk. He strode across and looked at the monitor. He saw her pull her phone out of her purse in a frantic gesture. The room had a signal blocker which meant she wouldn't be able to make or receive calls or messages or access internet services.

Bosco strode in a minute later. "Where is she?"

"In the interrogation room," he replied. "Let's go in."

He walked down the corridor and opened the door.

Joy jumped in her seat when she saw Bosco standing behind him.

Both of them walked in and sat on the bench across from her. Bosco didn't say anything. He didn't need to say anything. He had a very penetrating stare that unnerved people and made them talk even if they didn't want to.

Fifteen minutes later, they had the whole story from Joy taped on the voice recorder as well as on video.

Two men had arrived at Park Hotel a few days ago asking about Anuli. None of the other staff had talked but Joy had volunteered to take them to Anuli's house and show them because Anuli hadn't been at work. They hadn't found Anuli there. Since she didn't know where Tope lived, she couldn't take them there.

Yesterday, they'd missed Anuli as she'd left work early with Bosco. So today, she took them back to Anuli's house. But she'd seen Anuli on the street and pointed her out to the men where they'd grabbed her. Anuli had fought the men but she'd been overpowered with a sedative. The men had paid Joy and dropped her off along the way before leaving with Anuli. She hadn't seen the men since. She didn't know where the men were taking Anuli or why. But they mentioned that a man wanted to see her. She didn't know who the man was.

The way she'd crumbled and blurted out the story, Tope had believed her. She wasn't a criminal mastermind, just a vindictive opportunist.

Although they were no closer to finding Anuli, they had a good description of the men who took her and the car they were in.

When police officers arrived, Joy was handed over to them along with a copy of her confession. The police would put out a call for patrols to look out for the vehicle and the men. If they were still in Port Harcourt or surrounding areas, then they would be found.

Tope and Bosco couldn't wait around for the police. Bosco went to talk to his contacts while Tope visited a few people in the local criminal underworld. It seemed nobody knew anything about a kidnapping. Even the local kingpin got furious that someone would pull a stunt like that on his turf without settling him. They would all help to find Anuli even if to teach the kidnappers a lesson.

By the time Tope got home, the sun was already on its way up the next day. He walked into the bedroom and the sight of the made bed hit him like a truck. He clutched his midriff as his throat hurt.

He'd been in automatic mode since Anuli went missing. But coming home and having to face the reality that she wasn't here made him ache all over.

This was the day they'd planned to travel to Makurdi. Now their plans about Anuli's stepfather had to be put on hold until she was found.

He was going to find her alive and well. He clenched his fists and pressed his forehead to the wall. *God, I don't ask you for many things. Keep her alive. Please.*

Taking a huge gulp of air to loosen the tightness in his chest, he walked into the bathroom for a shower. He came out and was pulling on fresh clothes when he heard the sound of keys in the door.

His heart thumped and for a minute he thought it was Anuli. He rushed into the hallway and found Bosco coming in, phone pressed to his ear. The other man looked clean and in new clothes too.

Tope's heart sank and he nodded at Bosco before walking back into the room to finish dressing.

Bosco followed him and there was urgency to his words. "Hang on. You have to hear this."

Tope swivelled. "What is it?"

"It's Siki. He called to give an update from Makurdi. He thinks he saw Anuli."

Chapter Twenty-Two

Anuli woke to heat. Sweltering, uncomfortable heat that made sweat soak into her clothes making them stick to her body. Worse, her body ached with bruises from rolling and slamming into the sides of the vehicle every time they hit a bump or swerved. Something vile-tasting was stuffed in her mouth and she couldn't see anything but blackness in the black jute bag she seemed to be enclosed in. She couldn't use her hands. They were tied behind her back and her feet were lashed together too as if she were a slaughtered ram ready to be roasted.

Her body shook uncontrollably and she felt dizzy. She felt as if she would suffocate or black out again. For the first time since her ordeal started, she felt fear. Fear that she would never escape. Fear that she would never see Tope again. Or Bosco.

Was this how her life was going to end? When she was so close to happiness? She'd found two men who cared about her and were willing to help her fulfil all her life dreams. Was she never to catch a break?

Her right shoulder and hip hurt. She tried to roll over so she could put the weight on the other side but couldn't. She would have to hope she got jolted again by a pothole and perhaps she would turn over on the other side.

The car jolted to a stop and she hit the side again but didn't roll back. Then she heard a click and some light filtered into the bag. She was hefted out of the trunk. It had to be two people carrying her as one pair of hands held onto her feet and another pair held her shoulders.

They didn't take care as her body banged against the corners of walls and even the steps. It felt as if every part of her body was on fire. Finally, they tossed her onto a hard surface. She presumed it was a concrete floor.

She felt tension to the bag. It became loose. Cool air surrounded her toes. They'd taken her shoes off at some point before she was stuffed in the bag. Someone tugged the other end of the bag, scraping her body along the floor. The bag peeled off.

Suddenly, she was surrounded by light. Her eyes hurt and she squeezed them shut. Slowly, she opened them, blinking until they adjusted to daylight.

Daylight. Was it only yesterday that she'd been abducted? They'd travelled a long way it seemed as the car had been on the road for most of the night.

The two men who had taken her stood on either end as she tried to push off the cold concrete floor. The floor was hard and there was a pungent smell in the air that made her want to retch. She couldn't as her mouth was stuffed with a gag. She had to swallow down the bitter bile.

She panted, struggling to breathe just as she tried to figure out what was going on. These men didn't work for Joy. It all seemed too complicated. In any case, if they were Port Harcourt guys, then why did they have to travel for so long?

Could this be Telema's doing? He was the only other person Anuli had offended recently who would want revenge for Tope breaking his fingers.

The men left her on the floor and walked out of the room. The space was bare with nothing else in it but her.

Anuli scrapped her body on the floor as she wriggled and rolled until she hit the wall. Bracing her tied hands on the floor, she levered her body into a sitting position.

A shadow fell across the room. She glanced up and saw a man peeking into the room. He held a phone in his hands and lifted it up to his face as if he was taking pictures.

Her eyes widened and she tried to speak but he was gone already.

She growled in frustration and closed her eyes, feeling exhausted. Then she fell asleep.

She woke with a jerk when she heard footsteps. Blinking rapidly, she tried to sit up as she had slumped forward in sleep.

Her vision was blurry at first and she didn't see the faces of the men.

One of them, a middle aged man in a dark suit and white shirt, stepped forward and loomed over her.

Her heart stopped for a few seconds before exploding into a race in her chest. She knew that face. Could never forget the face.

"Welcome back, Anuli. It's been a very long time indeed," Uncle Joe said in an oily voice she recognised too well as he pulled her gag off.

The man she'd been running away from had found her. She'd known a day of reckoning would come. But she'd hoped to be the one with the upper hand on this occasion.

She tilted her head back and closed her eyes. She wouldn't let him see her fear. Not ever again.

"Hello, Uncle Joe," she replied in a tone filled with contempt. "I see you're still abducting people and keeping them against their will. But am I not a little too old for your usual type? I thought you like them still in diapers."

His eyes narrowed and he stepped forward and smacked her across the face. A coppery taste filled her mouth from where she bit her tongue.

"I have something special in store for you." His words felt like venom in her mind. "Someone is coming over soon to buy you. I'm going to make a very good price for you. You can call it your bride price. But you're not going to get a husband. Oh, no, my dear. You are being sold into the slave market and being shipped to Europe. I know the Italians like to fuck African prostitutes. Or perhaps you might even end up in London. I have an Albanian contact that can get you into a whore house over there."

He stepped back and pulled out a handkerchief and dabbed his sweaty forehead.

Anuli felt nauseous but she fought not to throw up. She panted as her chest hurt. She would not show fear. Not to him. She repeated to herself.

"Is that all? I'm looking forward to going to Europe." She feigned nonchalance. "It has to be better than Port Harcourt. But I'm curious. All these years you didn't bother with me. And all of a sudden you came to find me."

He sneered. "You think I didn't look for you. I cursed Chief for letting two tiny girls overpower him and run away. I sent men to search for you. No one found you anywhere. It wasn't until a few weeks ago when I found out that someone was investigating me that I started doing my own investigation. It was your meddling friend and her fiancé who led me to you. You don't think I got to my position in the police force for nothing. There's nothing that goes on around me that I don't know about."

Oh, no! It was Peter's investigation that had revealed Anuli's location. She hoped the security around Tessa was tight and that the man wouldn't end up kidnapping her too.

"So my dear, relax. You'll be out of my hair soon and the stupid investigation is not going to get anywhere. This thing runs a lot higher than you can ever know."

He swivelled and walked out of the room.

Despair gripped Anuli and she crouched against the wall as her body trembled.

Chapter Twenty-Three

Sergeants Idoko and Pelu sat on the steps outside the building where Anuli was being held prisoner. Between them were the bowls of Okoho soup with pounded yam that they had sent the constable manning the gates to buy for them. Two green bottles of Star beer sat on the top stair.

Pale moon light lit up the space. They had chosen to sit outside enjoying the cool breeze fluttering the leaves of the mango tree. There was a black out tonight with no electricity.

Idoko chewed the last piece of smoked fish from the soup as he looked up at the sky. A bank of cloud moved swiftly and it looked like it might rain later. He reached in his chest pocket and pulled out a packet of cigarettes.

He pulled one out before placing the pack on the floor. Pelu always took a stick from him even though the other man claimed he wasn't a smoker. But Idoko didn't hold it against the man. There were a lot of people who were in denial about a lot of things.

Himself notwithstanding.

As he expected, Pelu reached for the packet just as Idoko lit his cigarette.

"So how long do you think we'll be assigned to this job?" Idoko asked.

"As long as the ACP wants us here we'll be here," Pelu replied before lifting the beer bottle to his lips.

Officially, they were on duty, guarding the woman they had taken from Port Harcourt City. So they shouldn't be drinking alcohol.

But the woman was tied up and harmless, locked up in a dark room. She was hardly any threat.

Anyway, there were worse crimes, like the fact they had abducted a woman and driven her across several states against her will. The ACP was currently in his house enjoying an evening with his family while Pelu and Idoko were stuck out here.

"Is he really going to sell that girl like he threatened?" Idoko asked as he blew smoke into the air and it dissipated in the breeze.

"It's like you don't know the ACP well. He is very well connected. He is very good friend with the state governor. He can do whatever he wants. So if he says he's selling the woman. Then he's selling the woman."

The men drank and smoked. When they were done, they went into the car, lowered the seats and slept on them.

***

Tope followed the directions Siki had given him until he pulled up outside a fenced off house in the outskirts of Makurdi. He and Bosco had driven for most of the day to get up here as soon as possible. They had alternated the driving just so they didn't have to do more than quick rest stops.

The beam of the headlamps showed Siki's dark Toyota Corolla. The front driver side door opened and the man stepped out.

Tope killed the lights as the man walked back to his SUV. He pulled the back door open and got inside Tope's car.

Both Tope and Bosco turned around to face him.

"What's the latest?" Bosco asked.

"There are still two men inside. They have been drinking alcohol and are currently sleeping it off so shouldn't pose much resistance. The third man is the gateman who I bribed to let me know what was going on in there. He will let us in when we're ready to go. I told him we have to tie him up just so he can say we overwhelmed him."

"Do we know where Anuli is being held?" Tope asked.

"Yes, I have an outline of the floor plan." He pulled out a sheet of paper from his pocket.

Tope turned on the overhead lamp and bathed the interior in yellow light. All three men checked out the exits and access to where Anuli was being held in a room on the ground floor.

It was obvious the men in the house didn't think there was any threat coming which gave Tope and Bosco the element of surprise.

Tope assigned each man their roles and they picked up the weapons Bosco had acquired for the mission.

Four men stormed the house—Tope, Bosco, Siki and Jim. They overpowered Idoko and Pelu without much of a fight. The two men were found asleep inside the car. Siki and Jim were left to guard them while Tope and Bosco hurried into the house where they found Anuli curled up in a corner of the room, in the dark.

Tope felt nauseated just as pain hit the back of his throat.

Bosco was next to her on the floor first just as she startled awake.

"It's okay, babe," Bosco said as Tope knelt on the floor beside her.

"Oh, God, Tope." She launched into Tope's arms and started sobbing.

Tope's heart wrenched as he listened to her sobs. He held her tight, burying his head in her hair as Bosco cut the ropes tying her hands and legs.

When her hands were free, Tope scooped her up and carried her out while Bosco used his torch to light the way out of the house. He held her until he got into the back seat of his car. There he pulled one of the spare bottles of water.

"Anuli, drink." He encouraged her to lift her head and have a sip. She looked weak and tired. She probably hadn't had anything to eat or drink since she was taken.

She sipped some water slowly while he held her.

There was no doubt now. He was going to kill her stepfather.

Chapter Twenty-Four

Joseph Uwadiegwu stirred in bed and opened his eyes. The air conditioner in the room had stopped working. The bed sheets clung to his sweaty body as the windows were closed and not letting in any air. The curtains were shut so very little light came in from the moon.

He had been in a celebratory mood earlier and had drunk a lot of alcohol while out with his friends. He'd come home late and already his wife was asleep in her room. He had insisted she have her own room when they got married. She hadn't protested. She was a good little wife and didn't know what he got up to with her son when he took the child out on their male bonding outings.

He should get up and open the window but the effect of the alcohol in his system made him reluctant to move. He closed his eyes. It popped open again when he felt cold metal pressed against his temple. A dark shadow loomed over him.

"Wake up, Uncle Joe."

His breath locked in his throat and he didn't breathe.

That voice. It couldn't be. She was locked up in the remote house.

A shadow moved across the foot of the bed and stood in front of the window so that the moon gave it a silhouette. The person moved the curtains aside, bathing the room in moonlight.

He saw her then. A woman in dark jeans and top with a balaclava over her head with a gun pointed at him.

"Get up," a man ordered. The one with a gun to his head.

Joseph pushed both hands onto the mattress and levered his upper half off the bed so he was sitting.

"Who are you and how did you get in here?" he asked in a mix of annoyance and fear.

"Your guards are dead," the woman said. "Your wife and her son are safe. Not that you care about them. I've explained everything to them and she doesn't want anything to do with you for what you have done to her son."

Joseph gasped. "What do you mean?"

The woman stepped forward, gun still levelled at Joseph. "The boy told his mother about where you take him every weekend and what the men do to him. His mother wants you dead for what you have done. This time, you won't get away with it."

More sweat broke out on Joseph's body. His throat dried out and he swallowed hard.

"I don't know what you're talking about. I'm the Assistant Commissioner for Police. If you harm me, you won't get away with it." His voice shook as well as his body.

"Do you think I care? But you can be sure that I'm going to harm you and I'm going to get away with it. There's no one coming to save you."

Suddenly, two pairs of hands were holding him down, pinning him to the bed, darker shapes in the gloom.

Terror exploded through him. "Get off—" a rag was stuffed in his mouth.

His eyes bulged in the sockets as his panic rose and he froze when he saw something glinting in the low light. A knife.

"How many children did you rape?" the woman asked.

The knife dug into his thigh. He screamed, no sound came out from behind the gag in his mouth. The knife was pulled out and stabbed into another part of his thigh.

"Ever heard of death by a thousand cuts? That's how you're going to die. By bleeding out."

Just when he thought he'd caught his breath from one cut, another would slice through his flesh. They cut through his PJ and the sweat made each wound sting more.

"Do you want to live?" It was the man's voice again.

Joseph nodded his head vigorously.

Someone pulled the gag out of his mouth. They dragged him out of the bed and got him kneeling on the floor. The wound on his thighs ached like hell. One of them had a torch pointed at his face. He had to blink several times as the light blinded him. Another held a phone up, recording. Both of them still pointed guns at him.

"Now, I want you to name every person you dealt with who has molested a child."

Joseph shook his head.

P-taff. A suppressed gun shot hit the mattress behind Joseph. And he trembled.

"Last warning. Start speaking," the man said.

Joseph swallowed hard and nodded. "The list of men you want are on my phone listed under Golf Buddies."

One of the shadows picked up his phone from his bedside and held it up. With shaky fingers, Joseph unlocked it.

A gun shot rang out. The sound of it shocked Joseph before he felt the pain rip through his gut. He clutched his stomach as sticky liquid seeped through his fingers. He'd been shot in the stomach.

"You...shot me," he coughed out.

"He promised not to kill you. I didn't." The second man was now looming over him.

The second bullet hit Joseph in his chest. He collapsed on the floor as the shadows floated past him. He was left dying alone on the cold floor. Every time he opened his mouth to call for help, blood bubbled into his mouth making it taste of copper. The pain in his gut hurt more than anything he'd ever experienced. He lay there for hours. As they had said, no help came for him.

At some point, he realised he wasn't exactly alone. The ghost of every person he'd killed stood all around him, waiting for the moment he would join them so they could inflict their own brand of torture on him. Suddenly, he feared death.

Finally as the grey light of dawn filled the room, Joseph Uwadiegwu took his last breath.

Epilogue

A month later, Anuli stood in the bathroom in Tope's house brushing her teeth as she got ready for bed.

Soon after they'd returned from Makurdi, she'd moved her things to this house. This was now her home.

She'd also had to make a statement to the police about being abducted. Joy was still in police custody and would remain there until she was prosecuted in court. After what the kidnappers had done to Anuli, she had no sympathy for the other girl and the role she'd played in her abduction. Of course, the girl had already lost her job.

In her police statement, she'd only mentioned the two men who had kidnapped her and where they had taken her. She didn't say anything about Uncle Joe or how the man had met his end.

Of course, her stepfather's death had been a big deal at first and marked as an assassination. But the video with him confessing his crimes and naming his accomplices had surfaced online and a nationwide investigation into a paedophile ring was currently underway. One of the men named had been found dead under mysterious circumstances assumed to be suicide.

Anuli was glad that each of the paedophiles named would face justice one way or the other. Now she didn't have to look over her shoulders again.

For the first time since her mother died, she could describe herself as happy.

She'd registered for the new school session at university. Although she was without her best friend, she didn't miss Tessa as much as she'd thought she would. She had school friends.

But she also had her men. Tope and Bosco.

Anuli stepped out of the bathroom to find a shirtless Bosco leaning against the door post. His lips were curled in a lopsided smile that always made her heart race.

"The expression on your face says you're up to something." She smiled up at him.

"Perhaps I am." He took her hand and her skin tingled. He tugged her into the room and sat her on the bed. "I wanted to talk to you before Tope joins us."

"What's going on?" She slid her palm across his chest, touching the scars on his skin gently.

He placed his hand over hers, making her stop the downward trail. "I have to go away for a few weeks for a job."

"Oh, how long?" Due to the secretive nature of his job, she'd learned not to ask too many questions. She'd also known that he wouldn't always be around, which was why she tried to make the most of any time he was around.

"A month. Probably longer."

"You're going to be careful, aren't you? You're going to come back in one piece," she said in a serious tone, searching his face.

"I'm going to try. I'll be back as soon as I can."

She nodded, slid her arms around his neck and leaned in to kiss him. He let her in, his taste exploding in her mouth. She gasped as he trailed his mouth down her neck to her shoulder. Her body heated up as it always did in his presence.

She didn't hear Tope come in. Only felt his presence when the mattress depressed and his heat covered her back.

"You started without me." Tope's warm breath grazed her right ear.

"I was just warming her up," Bosco said in her left ear.

All of a sudden, it was as if they were two hulking, wrestling duo as they hauled her body into the middle of the bed without the towel that had been covering her from her shower.

Now she was spread out naked between them as they caressed her skin from top to bottom. She was breathless with excitement, her entire body vibrating with pleasure.

Bosco's fingers trailed down her legs, spreading her thighs apart. He was definitely the pussy lover around here. Always first to delve in there and get her panting with pleasure. But he didn't do anything. She looked up to find him exchange a grin with Tope. The two of them were definitely up to something.

"Come on, guys," she protested.

"Would you like Bosco to do something for you, Tiger?" Tope had a sexy grin on his face.

"Yes. I want both of you to do things to me. Things that make me go crazy and wet with want."

"Oh, she's a sweet talker, isn't she?" Bosco chuckled. "I can't refuse her anything."

Before she could reply, he'd settled between her spread thighs and went to town on her wet and throbbing pussy, his lips and tongue and teeth, stroking, nibbling, swirling.

At the same time, Tope descended on her hard and aching boobs, kneading the flesh and pinching the nipple on one even as he sucked on the other.

Arcs of desire bounced around her body, making it heat up and her skin tingle. She got lost in the moment. In these men. She knew she didn't want to live without one if not both of them. They loved her and she loved them. Not in the way other people loved. But then again, she wasn't other people. She would never be normal. But she didn't care.

As long as they loved her, nothing else matter.

"Oh, god," she cried out as Bosco hummed over her clit. Her body trembled as she raced towards an orgasm. Her fingers clawed at the sheets underneath as her body arched off the bed covered in sweat. She saw stars before collapsing back down on the bed, panting for breath.

She felt cool lube and then fingers dipped into her back hole. They weren't done with her. Her brain had already shut down and she was just a mass of sensation as Bosco lifted her over his naked body and thrust into her kitty, just as she felt the hard, heavy presence of Tope behind her, filling her up.

She shivered as her core tightened with pleasure. She wasn't far off from another orgasm and the coordinated effort from both men sent her shattering a second time before they found their release.

Her eyes were already dripping shut before the men pulled out of her and cleaned her up.

Later in the middle of the night, she woke and reached for Tope. He woke up, pulled her onto his chest.

"Are you okay?" he asked in the deep voice that she was now so used to and held his affection for her.

"You're not going to leave me, are you?" She didn't know why she needed to hear him say the words again.

"I'm never going to leave you, my love. Balogun men mate for life." He pulled back to look at her face.

His reassurance made warmth bloom in her chest. She leaned up and kissed his lips. "I'm glad you found me, Tope. I am yours forever."

Thank you for reading Captive. If you enjoyed this story, please leave a quick review on the site of purchase.

I offer my mailing list subscribers the chance to read previews of upcoming books before the release date. Make sure you don't miss out on the free reads, giveaways and news of upcoming book events by visiting my website www.kirutaye.com and signing up for my mailing list.

Until our next fictional adventure,
Kiru xx